THE SEVEN SIGNS

①

For Ava and Clare

Scholastic Australia
345 Pacific Highway, Lindfield NSW 2070
An imprint of Scholastic Australia Pty Limited
(ABN 11 000 614 577)
PO Box 579, Gosford NSW 2250
www.scholastic.com.au

Part of the Scholastic Group
Sydney • Auckland • New York • Toronto • London • Mexico City
• New Delhi • Hong Kong • Buenos Aires • Puerto Rico

Published by Scholastic Australia in 2016.
Text copyright © Michael Adams, 2016.
Cover design by Blacksheep Design Ltd UK.
Cover photography: Pyramids, Giza, Egypt © plainpicture/Design Pics – Chris Coe.
Cover copyright © Scholastic Australia, 2016.

Internal illustrations by Blacksheep Design Ltd UK.
Internal images: p4, mind atoms © istockphoto.com/agsandrew; p13 & various pages, infinity
© Absemetov/Shutterstock.com.

National Library of Australia Cataloguing-in-Publication entry

Creator: Adams, Michael Edwin, 1970- author.
Title: Skyfire / Michael Adams.
ISBN: 9781743628010 (paperback)
Series: Adams, Michael Edwin, 1970- Seven signs; 1.
Target Audience: For primary school age.
Subjects: Adventure stories.
Dewey Number: A823.4

Printed by McPherson's Printing Group, Maryborough, Victoria.

Scholastic Australia's policy, in association with McPherson's Printing Group, is to use papers
that are renewable and made efficiently from wood grown in responsibly managed forests,
so as to minimise its environmental footprint.

10 9 8 7 6 5 4 3 2 1   16 17 18 19 20 / 1

THE SEVEN SIGNS

(1)

SKYFIRE

MICHAEL ADAMS

A Scholastic Australia Book

The girl knew she was going to die. Her heart thumped. Mouth dry, throat tight, she could barely breathe. She looked at the madman with the gun, who'd trapped her, on top of a train hurtling through the night. There was no way she could get out of this alive. The next few seconds could go one of two ways. He would shoot her or she'd jump. Either way, it would be the same result. She'd be dead.

The girl didn't want to die, but she knew pleading for her life would be useless. The mad gleam in her pursuer's eyes told her that begging wouldn't change his mind.

The man moved closer, along the roof of the carriage. He walked casually, as if he wasn't scared of being in such a precarious position. His sneer said he was enjoying this, said he was savouring her last terrified moments.

Buffeted by the wind, arms seesawing for balance, the girl backed away as the train swayed along the tracks.

'There's nowhere to go,' he yelled, following, his pistol aimed right at her heart. 'You know that, don't you?'

The girl glanced behind her. Her stomach dropped and her heart hammered harder. The heels of her sneakers were wobbling over the edge of the deadly gap between the train carriages. Another inch or bump and she'd fall, get sucked beneath the train, be thrown under dozens of steel wheels. Somehow that seemed an even worse fate than being shot or jumping to her death.

The train lurched. The girl screamed and staggered, fearing the worst—arms flailing, fighting for balance. She tipped, fell forwards and landed hard on her knees, grabbing hold of the pipes that ran along the edge of the carriage roof so she didn't slide off. In that brief moment, the girl felt a flash of hope. Maybe the train's sudden movement had surprised her pursuer, sent him toppling from the train. But when she looked up, the man still stood steady as a statue before her.

'On your feet!' He waved her up with the gun barrel. 'Now!'

The girl got up swaying, trying to be brave even as she stared at the certain death promised by the look on his horrible face.

'Things didn't have to be this way,' he shouted, shaking his head in mock regret as the train howled past a deserted railway station. 'You could have lived!'

The girl flinched. This was it. Her heart felt like it was going to burst. She looked around desperately, as though an escape portal might magically appear. Who was she kidding?

The moonlit landscape flashed by. The train was going so fast and she knew if she jumped it would take the authorities, or anyone, ages to find her—once they even realised she was missing. But she had no choice. She took a deep breath and tried to tell herself it was like diving into a cold swimming pool. Once she leaped, it would be too late to turn back. Everything would be over in a second.

As if reading her mind, the man snapped his pistol up so its ghastly black muzzle pointed right at her face.

'There's nowhere to hide this time,' he shouted. 'You're going to die.'

Dazzle us with your genius!
Enter the DARE Awards...
and make your dreams come true!

SEVEN WINNERS WILL HAVE THEIR LIVES
CHANGED IN AMAZING WAYS!
FOR YOUR CHANCE TO BE ONE OF THEM,
TELL US ABOUT YOUR BIGGEST AMBITIONS
AND WHY THEY MEAN SO MUCH TO YOU.

ENTRY IS FREE AND OPEN TO PEOPLE AGED 10 TO 17.

Zander had dreamed, he had dared, and now his whole world was about to change forever. It was exhilarating. His stomach swirled and turned like a roller-coaster. But he needed to keep himself under control. The other winners would be here soon and it wouldn't be a good look, letting on just how much all of this meant to him, being in New York as a winner of the DARE competition, waiting in the backstage guest room to receive his award from charismatic trillionaire Felix Scott.

He had come a long way from the carefree boy he'd been before the sudden loss of his parents. Zander would have gladly traded all of this to have them back. But he hoped in being selected as a DARE Award winner they would have been proud of what he had achieved.

'This is for you both,' he said under his breath.

Zander allowed himself a smile. This was also for his grandfather, now seated somewhere in the ballroom of Felix's Infinity Hotel. The old man could be a rascal, but he'd made life less lonely in their big house back in Athens.

When Zander checked his tie in the wall mirror, he saw a handsome young man, with amber eyes, chiselled features and hair as dark as midnight falling in ringlets to the collar of his charcoal suit. He nodded approvingly at his reflection. Soon he would be standing not just in front of his grandfather, but also in front of the city's biggest celebrities and richest citizens to receive the award—all covered by the world's media. Zander knew in his heart of hearts he deserved this.

On wobbly legs, a freckle-faced girl wearing a green headscarf and a silky red dress walked into the plush room and caught Zander's eye. 'Hello,' she said. 'I'm a DARE winner. My name is Yasmin. I do not wear usually high heels.' She smiled, putting out her arms, pretending to balance.

'Zander. I'm a DARE winner, too. Very good to meet you,' he said, gesturing at a table laden with platters of gourmet food. 'I was just thinking this seems too good to be true.'

'As delicious as it all looks, I do not think I can eat,' said Yasmin, pointing to her stomach. 'Butterflies.'

'Me, too,' he said with a grin. 'It really is—'

'Yo!'

Yasmin was startled and nearly toppled out of her unfamiliar shoes. Zander turned with a scowl, unhappy to be interrupted, and saw a boy with a riot of sandy hair lope into the lounge. The intruder's white high-top sneakers hinted that he didn't feel he belonged in his black suit.

'Wassup?' he said, blue eyes twinkling. 'I'm Andy.'

'My name is Yasmin,' said the girl formally. 'I am from Egypt. And this is Zander from ... ?'

'Greece,' Zander said abruptly, narrowing his eyes at Andy as he folded his arms and drew himself up to his full height. 'Athens.'

'Cool,' Andy replied brightly, unfazed by Zander's

manner. 'I'm from Hell-A, also known as Los Angeles.' He let out an appreciative whistle as his eyes travelled across the room's priceless artwork and expensive furniture. 'Wow, this crib is totally rad, huh?'

Zander rolled his eyes at Andy's Californian way of talking. Amused, Yasmin suppressed a little smile.

'So,' Zander said, frowning at the American, '*you* won a DARE Award?'

If Andy caught his tone, he didn't let on. 'That's what they tell me, my man.'

'Um, am I in the right place?' A dark-skinned boy with short dreadlocks hovered in the doorway. He blinked behind expensive glasses and tugged at the collar of his brown suit jacket.

'You are if you won a DARE Award,' said Andy. 'I'm Andy.'

The new boy smiled at the warm welcome. 'I'm Dylan.'

'Dude, your accent?' Andy said. 'Aussie?'

Dylan nodded. 'Well spotted, mate.'

Andy laughed. 'I'm from LA. Zeus there is from Greece.'

'Ignore him if you can,' Zander said, scowling at Andy as he shook hands with Dylan. 'I'm Zander.'

'Easier said than done,' Andy said. 'Anyway, Yasmin here's from Egypt.'

'Sweet,' Dylan said, smiling at her. 'I went there one time with my parents.'

'You did?' asked Yasmin brightly. 'I live right near the—' She was distracted by the arrival of a girl with pink hair in a blue dress, a silver stud in her nose and chunky silver bracelets clattering at her wrists.

'Welcome, number five!' Andy said cheerfully as the girl strode confidently into the lounge in her red boots.

She nodded. '*Hola*, I'm Isabel.'

As they introduced themselves, another girl slipped in quietly. Her black bob framed a pale face set with startling emerald eyes. White arms folded defensively against her black lace dress, the new arrival averted her gaze to a painting of a dripping clock.

Isabel smiled at the others. 'Shy,' she mouthed, before crossing to stand by the new girl. 'I love this guy's paintings,' she said. 'I'm Isabel. And you are?'

'Mila,' the girl answered in a small voice, still staring ahead. 'Mila Cortez.'

'Cortez?' Isabel said. '*¿De dónde eres?*'

Mila looked her way, unfolded her arms and replied softly in Spanish.

'You *habla Español* or whatever?' Dylan whispered to the others.

'A little,' Yasmin said. 'I learn in my family tourist shop. She is telling Isabel she is living at the Chilean base in Antarctica.'

'The South Pole?' Andy said, grinning. 'No wonder she hasn't got much of a tan.'

'Everyone,' came a woman's clipped voice from the other side of the room, 'your attention please.'

All eyes turned to the elegant Eurasian woman in the

doorway. Each of the DARE Award winners had met Felix Scott's executive assistant, Miss Chen, when they'd arrived at the Infinity Hotel that afternoon. She was tall and poised in her pinstripe suit, black hair smoothly chic in a perfect bun. Miss Chen's feline eyes flitted behind SmartGlasses and dipped constantly to her tablet. She gave off an air of being so efficient that she could do three things at once.

'This is Jae-joon from South Korea,' she said, stepping aside for an Asian boy with artfully arranged hair and a funky Seoul Man T-shirt, worn with his trendy white suit.

'Hello,' Jae-joon said, offering a little bow. 'Please, call me JJ.'

'Perfect,' Miss Chen said, 'that is all of you. Please, make yourselves comfortable. I will return to escort you to the stage in ten minutes.'

With that she was gone, closing the door behind her.

An awkward silence descended.

Andy cleared his throat. 'So, first there were the dwarfs and then the magnificent—and now here we are!'

The others looked at him like he was crazy.

'Get it?' Andy grinned. 'The Seven Dwarfs? The Magnificent Seven? Now look out world, because we're . . . the DARE Seven!'

While Zander gave another eye roll, the rest of the group burst out laughing. With the ice broken, they stood around the buffet table, picking at food and chatting about how amazing the Infinity Hotel was and how cool it had been to get new clothes for the award ceremony.

'Do you guys think,' Andy said around a mouthful of cheese, 'that we'll be given, like, actual prizes?'

'What is it you are thinking?' Isabel asked.

Andy shrugged. 'Felix Scott's the richest man in the world. The sky's the limit. Use your imagination.'

As Zander frowned, JJ let out a chuckle. 'Yup,' he said, 'I'll take a submarine—made of gold!'

'I'll take any of the artworks in this room,' Isabel said.

Dylan raised a hand. 'Put me down for one of Felix's new flying cars.'

'Totally,' Andy agreed. 'Hey, so what about you, Zan?'

'Zander,' he corrected, 'just Zander.'

'OK, *just Zander*,' Andy said, teasing, 'what do *you* want from Felix?'

The Greek boy pointed at a wall screen showing footage of how Felix Scott had made Infinity Corporation into the biggest company in the world. 'Surely the real prize is the opportunity to meet him.'

Andy rolled his eyes. 'Way to bring the mood down.'

But Yasmin frowned. 'No, Andy, he is right. How many people get to spend time with the "Internet King"?'

Zander shot her a nod.

'I know he's amazing and everything,' said JJ, now peering down through a window, 'but that doesn't mean everyone's a fan. Check it out.'

They all went over to the window. On the autumnal streets beneath the hotel, protestors held up placards and chanted, their voices too faint to make out the words.

'"Infinity wrecks the planet",' Dylan read aloud, squinting to read a sign.

'That one says "Infinity steals ideas",' added Yasmin.

'These things, are they true?' Mila asked.

Zander shrugged. 'You can't make an omelette without breaking eggs.'

'What does this mean, about the omelette?' Mila asked.

'It means successful people always have a lot of enemies,' Andy explained. 'Why, I myself have made quite a few ene—'

A whoosh cut him off. Everyone spun around as a life-size 3D hologram of the purple-haired, purple-clothed Avarava—the world's most famous pop star—was streamed live into the room's HoloSpace from her performance in the ballroom next door.

'Welcome to the DARE Awards!' her hologram called out. 'We're going to have a great night!'

As Avarava launched into her hit song, *Best Behava*, the room's wall screens showed starstruck adults in tuxedos and gowns jumping up from their tables to sing along.

'Do we get to meet her?' JJ asked excitedly.

'Please tell me we do!' Isabel added.

Mila blinked. 'This singer, she is famous?'

'You *have* heard of Avarava, right?' Andy said.

Mila blushed. 'The name is familiar, but her songs, no.'

'But you *do* have music in Antarctica?' Andy joked.

'I like the classical music,' Mila replied. 'Mozart, Beethoven. You *have* heard of them, yes?'

Andy laughed. Mila was shy but it looked like she had a

sly sense of humour, too. 'I love those dudes,' he shot back. 'Especially their new stuff!'

Mila grinned that she got the joke and the others smiled—even Zander.

On the ballroom stage, Avarava finished her song.

'Thank you!' the pop princess shouted, blowing kisses and taking a bow. 'Thank you, I love you all!'

The crowd cheered and cheered.

'Right now,' Avarava said when the applause died down, 'I am very pleased to introduce the man who changed my life when he signed me to his record label, Infinity Music, all those years ago. And now he's about to change the lives of more lucky young people.'

In the guest lounge, the DARE Award winners traded nervous glances.

'Ladies and gentlemen,' Avarava continued, 'please welcome the founder of Infinity Corporation and a true twenty-first century visionary, the amazing Felix Scott!'

Amid thunderous applause, Felix Scott ran onto the stage. In the guest lounge, his hologram kissed Avarava's cheek before she moved offstage and left him alone in the spotlight. With his blue eyes, mane of white hair and trademark crimson suit, Felix was often said to look like a younger, slimmer and more handsome Santa Claus. But he really *was* like Santa in that he could make just about any dream come true.

'DARE,' Felix boomed in his British accent. 'It stands for my personal motto—"Dream! Act! Realise *Everything*!"

Tonight we're here to celebrate some very special young people who are already on their way to doing just that!'

Felix turned to a giant screen where the endless loop of the Infinity logo gleamed.

Then letters swirled in a jumble before forming the words of the DARE Awards advertisement. 'Four months ago, I sent out this message. "Dazzle us with your genius",' he read. '"Enter the DARE Awards".' Felix smiled brightly at the audience. 'I placed this ad in newspapers and magazines, on websites and social media, all around the world. There was no mention of me or what prizes there might be. I didn't want entrants telling me what they thought I'd want to hear or what they thought would make them rich. Honest answers about their dreams and ambitions—*that's* what I was looking for. But I was also looking for more. I wanted young people who weren't just dreamers, but *doers*.'

Felix paced the stage, seeming to make eye contact with everyone in the ballroom.

'As a child living in poverty,' he said, 'I didn't just *dream* about a better life—I decided to *do* what I could to make one for myself. First computer program at age seven. Infinity Search Engine at fourteen. Billionaire by twenty-one. At twenty-eight, I was employing over one million people in a hundred and fifty countries. By the time I was thirty-five, Infinity was the biggest company on Earth, and at forty-two I became the world's first trillionaire. I only realised this year, when I turned forty-nine, that all the major landmarks in my life have occurred at seven-year intervals. To celebrate, I created the DARE Awards to give seven young dreamers and doers the chance to make a real difference to the world!'

Felix paused as the spotlight settled on the parents and guardians of the DARE Award winners, seated at the VIP table nearest the stage. 'Please join me in congratulating the wonderful people who've raised tonight's guests of honour,' he said warmly.

Polite clapping suddenly became thunderous cheering in the ballroom as A-list movie stars Kit and Katlyn Taylor swept theatrically up the central aisle. Waving to the applauding crowd, the celebrity couple, known worldwide simply as 'KitKat', took the two seats that had been glaringly empty at the VIP table.

'Making it about them as always,' Dylan said grumpily from the lounge. 'Thanks heaps, Mum and Dad.'

'What?' Andy asked, wide-eyed. 'You're Dylan *Taylor*?'

JJ clicked his fingers. 'Your face, I knew it was familiar!'

'This KitKat, even I know of them,' said Mila. '*Galactic Quest*—I love this movie.'

Isabel smiled. 'Me, too!'

'Yup,' JJ said excitedly. 'It's the best. They're really your mother and father?'

'I'm adopted,' Dylan sighed. 'Guess I'm just lucky like that.'

Zander arched an eyebrow. Yasmin caught his glance and they shared a secret headshake, both unimpressed by celebrity.

Miss Chen reappeared at the backstage door and switched off the HoloSpace, the room seeming suddenly empty minus the lifelike 3D image. 'Perfect,' she said into her SmartGlasses before focusing on the DARE Award winners. 'It is time. Is everyone ready?'

The winners exchanged skittish looks.

'Perfect,' she said. 'Come then.'

'Without any further ado,' Felix boomed, 'please welcome the seven winners of the DARE Awards!'

As the crowd roared and news drones hovered, the group walked onto the dazzlingly bright stage and shook hands with Felix before lining up beside him.

'Congratulations to you all,' he said when the applause had died down. 'It's a genuine pleasure to meet seven of the best and brightest hopes for the future of our world!'

Nervous and proud, the DARE Award winners beamed out at the sea of faces.

Felix rubbed his hands together, like he was getting down to business. 'So,' he said, smiling. 'My guess is you'd like to know *what* prizes I can offer?'

Zander couldn't evade Andy's told-you-so grin.

'A question like that *did* come up,' Andy wisecracked.

Felix laughed. 'I'm giving each of you a chance at fame, money and adventure. And that includes...'

Time seemed to slow down. Zander could hear his heart beating in his ears. He bet the others could, too.

'New InfiniFones with unlimited lifetime accounts,' Felix said.

The group looked at each other excitedly. The company's phones were the hottest items on the market.

'Plus, you'll get to try Infinity Air's brand-new Space-Skimmer ultra-fast jets!' Felix continued. 'You're each getting a seven-day world-travel open ticket that'll give you a chance to visit each other and get to know your fellow winners!'

Excited gasps filled the hotel ballroom. Felix's ultra-fast jets flew at the edge of space! Felix raised a hand to quiet down the audience's enthusiasm.

'Then I'd like to invite you to join me for seven days aboard the biggest, most technologically advanced vessel on the ocean...'

The air pressure in the ballroom seemed to increase.

'...the *Infinite Horizon*.'

The teens traded high fives as the ballroom broke out in applause once again.

Felix grinned. 'So, I take it you've all heard of my boat?' he asked.

They nodded eagerly. Calling *Infinite Horizon* a *boat* was a crazy understatement. It was a floating city that was an invitation-only destination for the world's richest, smartest, most famous and powerful people.

'On board the *Infinite Horizon*, you'll get to talk about your ideas and plans with some of the best and brightest minds on the planet. Writers, inventors, doctors, scientists, artists, programmers, filmmakers, astronauts and more, will all share their experiences and advice with you. My hope is you'll find the mentors you need to grow and achieve your dreams.'

The crowd cheered.

Felix held up a hand. The audience simmered down.

'There's one last thing I should mention,' the trillionaire said.

The ballroom was so quiet, Zander was sure he could hear champagne fizzing in crystal flutes.

Ever the showman, Felix let the moment stretch. 'At the end of our time together on the *Infinite Horizon*, I'm going to give each of you . . .'

He looked at seven expectant faces.

'. . . one . . . million . . . dollars!'

The Infinity Hotel ballroom erupted into a frenzy.

A SPECIAL NEWS REPORT

Who DARES wins!

Seven lucky teenagers are on top of the world after trillionaire Felix Scott named them as the winners of his DARE Awards in a glittering ceremony at the Infinity Hotel last night. The teens will each receive $1 million, spend a week flying around the world on Infinity Air's new SpaceSkimmers, enjoy another week on the *Infinite Horizon*, and be able to keep in touch with each other for life on free InfiniFones.

Here's the lowdown on the lucky seven prize winners.

Two years ago, American skater **Andy Freeman, now 15**, set up *Scoop*, a blog where he publishes investigative stories exposing criminals who rip off kids. 'My dream is to build *Scoop* into a worldwide network where kids can publish their own articles and become investigative journalists, too,' says Andy. Andy's dad, a decorated LA cop, couldn't hide his tears when his son dedicated his award to his late mother. 'She was a really brave reporter.'

Born in Haiti, **Dylan Taylor, also 15**, lives in Australia with his superstar parents, A-list movie stars Kit and Katlyn Taylor—

better known as KitKat. A self-confessed 'underwater nerd', Dylan is a future marine biologist. 'Only five percent of the ocean has been mapped,' he says. 'My dream is to explore the secrets of the sea and encourage people to save its species and habitats.'

Fourteen-year-old Yasmin Adib greets customers at her parents' tourist shop in Cairo, Egypt with the question, 'What makes you happy?' Her LiveFoto recordings of their answers adorn the shop walls and her website, Yasminshappinessproject.com. 'My dream is to get answers from people all over the earth,' she says. 'I think showing how similar we are can help make a more peaceful world.'

You may not have heard of Greece's **Zander Demeter, 16,** but chances are you love *NEO Avenger*, the asteroid-smashing, free game app he created. The app also gives NASA access to the unused computing power of millions of devices to help it search for real asteroids that could destroy the earth. 'My goal is to develop more fun apps but also protect humanity from the many other threats we face,' explains Zander.

Isabel Garcia, 15, grew up in a tough part of Bogotá, Colombia. Her viral video campaign, *Libros no Armas* (Books not Guns), encourages local kids to take a pledge to stay at school and refuse to join gangs. More than ten thousand kids have made videos. 'School attendance is on the rise,' says Isabel. 'The criminals aren't happy but I don't care and I won't back down. I want kids in Colombia to have the same opportunities as everywhere else.'

Maths genius **Mila Cortez, 14,** lives with her parents at the Chilean base in Antarctica, one of less than a hundred people to have ever been born in the South Pole region! Her dream is just as out of this world: to be the first person on Mars. 'Already I discovered a new planet using the telescope of the base,' she says. 'I even got to name it after my favourite ballet— Planet Nutcracker!'

From Seoul, South Korea, **Park Jae-joon**, or **JJ, 15**, lost the use of his legs in a car accident when he was two. But he can now walk and run faster than most boys his age, thanks to the advanced robotic leg mecha he designed for himself! Now he wants to use his inventing skills to make a better world. 'My goal is to invent medi-bots to help people in countries where there aren't enough doctors,' JJ says.

Listening to her father's pigeons coo softly in their rooftop aviary, Yasmin sat with her journal on her lap, looking out at the Great Pyramid and its two smaller sisters shimmering against the desert horizon. The streets below Giza's sprawl of low-rise buildings bustled with traffic as hawkers and hustlers went about their business to the constant soundtrack of honking horns. Even on a Sunday, Giza, like the rest of Cairo, was always moving, always noisy.

Yasmin smiled to think of everyone going about their normal activities on a day that was going to be anything but normal for her. Today she would take her first Space-Skimmer flight, shooting up into the upper atmosphere over the Mediterranean, before landing in Athens so she could visit Zander for a few days. She couldn't believe the day had finally arrived. Her adventure was about to begin!

But first Yasmin had to pack. She put her journal down on the side table, got up and went down the stairs to her little bedroom. As always, her eyes drifted to the walls. Like the ceiling of her family's shop on the ground floor, she had covered them with hundreds of LiveFotos. Yasmin smiled as she thought about how she could use her DARE Awards prize money to travel to every country in the world and ask everyone she met, 'What makes you happy?' She imagined a day when Yasminshappinessproject.com could become a

TV series that would help turn the world into a more understanding and peaceful place. But that was in the future.

Right now, she wanted to prepare a smart look for when she arrived in Athens. Yasmin combed her long brown hair and put on her favourite jade shirt, blue jeans and her sneakers. 'Yes, that will do it,' she said to her reflection.

Yasmin picked up her InfiniFone from where she had left it charging overnight. She smiled as she read through the new comments visitors had posted to her website.

But what was more puzzling was the odd text message that had come through sometime in the night, from an unknown number.

The symbol must be some sort of strange spam, Yasmin thought.

'You look like you're a million miles away already,' her grandmother, Radha, said, up from the shop, where she often helped out, charming the customers.

Yasmin looked up from her phone. 'Do you need help in the store?'

Radha shook her head. 'Just a few people browsing. Mahmoud can handle it.'

Yasmin smiled. 'Of this you are sure, Grandmother?'

'I told him he must stay behind the counter,' Radha said with a cheeky grin. 'And keep his oven mitts on!'

It was a familiar joke. Mahmoud was many things—gentle, generous and protective of his little sister—but he was also clumsy. And that wasn't great when the family store was filled with delicate plaster and glass souvenirs. But Mahmoud was only clumsy when he was on two legs. Put him on two wheels and he was the best Cleopatra Pizza motorbike delivery driver in the whole of Cairo. His daredevil riding style was a constant source of worry for their parents, but for Mahmoud his job meant he got paid to practise the skills he would need to achieve his ultimate dream of becoming a movie stuntman.

'Anyway, it's not for long,' Radha continued. 'Your parents will be back soon.'

'And just where are Mum and Dad?' Yasmin asked.

'Secret mission,' Radha said, mischievous old eyes on the pile of clothes and empty suitcase on her granddaughter's bed. 'Just don't pack yet, OK?'

'What does that mean?' Yasmin said. 'Tell me!'

Her grandmother shook her head. 'Come here,' she said, arms outstretched. 'I'm going to miss you, child.'

'I'll miss you, too, Grandmother,' Yasmin said, hugging her tight.

Radha held her a moment longer. 'Can I ask you just one favour?'

'Of course.'

'Take me with you!'

Yasmin laughed. 'I wish I could.'

Radha reached into her pocket, pulled out a small glass vial filled with sand and handed it to her granddaughter.

'What is this?' Yasmin enquired.

'A little bit of home to take with you wherever you

go,' Radha said. 'If you really do get homesick, you can pour some sand out and always feel Egypt between your fingers—or toes!'

Yasmin grinned. 'Thank you, Grandmother.'

They hugged again. Radha pulled free, eyes twinkling. 'I'll go and make us some tea.'

Yasmin smiled at the sound of one of her grandmother's beloved action movies coming from the little wind-up TV she kept in the kitchen. But her amusement soured when she heard angry voices downstairs.

'Oh, Mahmoud,' Yasmin sighed, picturing him tripping over something breakable. 'What have you done now?' She rushed down the stairs and through the beaded doorway at the back of the shop.

Her mouth dropped open at what she saw.

Three uniformed policemen were shooing tourists away from the store's front door. Another one reached up to spray-paint the lens of the store's security camera. But worst of all, an older man in a suit and mirrored sunglasses held Mahmoud up against the wall by the throat.

'Hey!' Yasmin cried. 'What's going on?'

Dylan's head was still spinning when the SpaceSkimmer touched down in LA after its short flight from Sydney. It was hard to believe he had flown halfway around the world in just three hours—and in a plane that nearly went all the way to space! He gripped his backpack and stepped out of the Infinity Air terminal into the cool LA evening.

Blinking in the harsh brightness of the city lights, he saw Andy grinning at him from the kerb, looking every inch the rad skater in his black long-sleeved shirt, camouflage pants and high-top sneakers. Dylan suddenly felt a bit daggy, and chilly, in his Hawaiian shirt, khaki trousers and boat shoes.

'G'day, mate!' Andy hollered in a fake Aussie accent. 'Welcome to LA!'

Dylan grinned. 'Yo, like, totally hello, dude,' he drawled in an equally terrible American accent.

The boys burst out laughing and high-fived.

Their driverless AutoTaxi hummed along the Pacific Coast Highway, passing airport hotels, gas stations, fast-food joints and the seesawing metal towers that pumped oil from beneath Los Angeles.

'So—the SpaceSkimmer flight?' Andy said. 'Spill!'

'A-may-zing,' Dylan enthused. 'You go weightless for a

second! And above the plane, it's black like space! And you can see all across the earth for hundreds of kilometres! And the InvisiLounge! Oh, mate, it's … it's … fully sick.'

Andy's blue eyes sparkled with mirth. '"Fully sick"? I assume that means "totally awesome" in Aussie speak?'

Dylan nodded as his phone beeped with a new message. 'Probably just another fan, texting me a love poem,' he joked. 'How many have you got now, mate?'

'Just as many as you!' Andy shot back, pulling out his InfiniFone. 'Then there are the weirdos who send through stuff I can't even understand.'

'Like what?' Dylan asked, intrigued.

'Like this,' Andy said, turning his phone screen so his friend could see the strange symbol that had arrived that afternoon.

Dylan held up his own phone. 'Mate, I got one of those, too.'

Andy looked at Dylan's screen.

'Unknown number?' he asked.

Dylan nodded.

'When did you get yours?'

'Just before I flew out of Sydney. I thought it was spam.'

'Do the pictures mean anything to you?' Andy asked.

'I might speak Aussie, but I don't speak "random symbols and numbers",' Dylan replied. 'How 'bout you?'

Andy shook his head. With a quick swipe, he copied his

symbol and searched the internet for a match.

'Hmm,' he said. 'Now that is totally whack.'

Scouring all the electronic knowledge in the world had returned just a single result—www.gamesthinker.com.

'Did you just find "games thinker"?' asked Dylan, who was searching his image, too.

'Yep. Open site,' Andy told his phone and a webpage flashed onto his screen.

The seconds ticked down as they watched.

'What's it counting down to?' Dylan asked.

'I haven't got a clue,' Andy said, 'and I *hate* that feeling.'

Before he could muse further, Dylan cried, 'Whoa, check that out!' pointing out the back window. 'That's what I want!'

Andy saw what he was talking about. An Infinity Transport flying-car prototype, sleek and golden, like an aerodynamic teardrop, was floating through the air above the cluster of yachts moored at Marina Del Ray.

'Felix's people have been testing them around the city for the past few months,' he said.

Dylan nodded. 'It would've been cool if we could've

gotten one of those to take us to Laguna Beach.' He rubbed his hands together excitedly. 'Mate, I can't wait to get in the water tomorrow.'

During their 3D hologram chats via HoloSpace in the month since the DARE Awards, Dylan and Andy had planned to head to Laguna Beach, just south of LA, to snorkel. Dylan was desperate to see the incredible reef and sea life and show his new mate what snorkelling was all about.

'That's tomorrow's fun, but tonight, we've got bigger fish to fry ...' Andy said.

'OK,' Dylan chuckled, 'what's bigger than me swimming with leopard sharks?'

Andy grinned. 'I'm onto a new *Scoop* story. This guy— Ethan—came to see me today. He needs help because some hacker creeps threatened to ruin all his school grades unless he pays them serious money.'

'Well, that sucks.'

'It does . . . except we're not going to let him get ripped off like that.'

'Hang on!' Dylan said, looking at Andy over the rims of his glasses. 'Did you say *we*? As in you and me, "we"?'

Andy nodded excitedly.

Dylan frowned. While it was cool that *Scoop* stories had put criminals behind bars, he shuddered to think what would happen if Andy ever got caught by the bad guys. 'You sure this Ethan guy really needs your—*our*—help?'

'Yeah, but wait 'til you hear what he has to say.' Sensing his friend's nerves, Andy flashed a reassuring grin. 'Don't worry, dude, it's not gonna be dangerous.'

Dylan laughed. 'Famous last words. OK, what do we have to do?'

The AutoTaxi pulled up outside the bungalow Andy shared with his father, a few blocks from Santa Monica beach.

'I'll get us some drinks,' Andy said as he went into the kitchen. 'Take a seat.'

That was easier said than done in the cluttered lounge room. Dylan cleared some books to make space on the couch. While he waited, he took the opportunity to look around. Shelves were piled high with crime thrillers. The coffee table was strewn with police journals. Framed pictures lined the mantelpiece, most featuring a smiling woman Dylan guessed was Andy's mum.

'Here we go,' Andy said, handing his guest an ice-cold cola before he sat cross-legged on the carpet. 'Play Ethan, log.' A wall screen lit up. 'I always record my interviews,' Andy explained. 'It's something I learned from my mum.'

'Uh, OK,' said Ethan in the video. 'Where do I start?'

He looked only a bit older than Andy and Dylan, with curly red hair. Squinting through thick glasses he shuffled in the very seat Dylan was now in as he sipped a cola nervously. Dylan looked at the table next to him and, sure enough, an empty bottle stood next to his full one.

'Just start at the beginning,' Andy said off-camera. 'Relax, this will be OK.'

Ethan nodded, reassured. 'So I got this email with a video file,' he said. 'I didn't recognise the address, but it looked like it might be from my school. When I played the video, I saw a computer screen with an official-looking page from the California Department of Education, and my junior school grades were being changed from As and Bs to Fs and then back again. Then they were redone and undone again. I think it was to show me how easy it'd be,' Ethan said, voice cracking. 'And at the end, this digitised voice said my grades would be ruined forever unless I delivered one thousand dollars in a plain envelope to Griffith Observatory tonight. I'm supposed to hide it in a couch and then clear out. And they said if I told my parents or called the cops, there'd be "consequences".' Ethan's voice became high-pitched. 'My future could be trashed. My folks worked their butts off to give me a good education. It'll all be for nothing if I can't graduate with high marks and get into university.' Ethan broke down into sobs.

'Did he show you the email?' Dylan asked Andy when the recording ended.

'He said it wiped itself as soon as he'd read it,' Andy said.

Dylan let out a low whistle. 'Mate, those are some pretty sophisticated bullies,' he observed. 'Even if Ethan pays them off now, who's to stop them asking for more money later?'

'Or doing the same thing to other kids,' added Andy. 'That's why we're going to stop them by exposing their scam on *Scoop*.'

Dylan got to his feet and paced. 'But how? How are we

going to get that sort of cash by tonight?'

'One step ahead of you,' Andy said. 'I've already got it.'

Dylan looked at Andy with wide eyes.

'Ethan handed it over when he stopped blubbering,' said Andy. 'He said he'd been working after school, and had emptied his savings account to pay these guys off. We marked it with lemon juice so it can be traced.'

Dylan nodded, impressed. 'Can I see it?'

'Sorry, bro, Ethan insisted on sealing the envelope before he left,' Andy said. 'For a guy who wanted my help, he was a bit untrusting! But it was all of his money so I guess I get where he was coming from. I've got it here, ready to go.' Andy held up a yellow envelope.

'OK, so now what?' Dylan asked, nervous and excited.

'Now,' Andy said, 'we've got just enough time to get ourselves to Griffith Observatory and set the trap!'

'Hey!' Yasmin cried again.

One of the cops hung the 'Closed' sign in the front window as Mahmoud's attacker grinned at Yasmin.

'Let him go!' she demanded.

'As you wish,' the man who seemed to be the leader replied, releasing her brother so he fell to the floor with a thump. He took a step towards Yasmin.

'Wh-wh-who are you?' she stammered.

'I'm a detective,' he said, flashing a badge from inside his suit jacket. 'These are my men. Do what I say and everything will be all right.'

The sick feeling in Yasmin's stomach screamed that he was lying about the second bit. Her instincts told her to tread carefully. 'What's your name?'

The detective leered at her with a horrible smile. He had stained teeth and his breath stank of cigarette smoke. He glanced at a statue of the dog-headed god, Anubis, standing beside him. 'You can call me Jackal.'

'Wh-wh-what do you want?' Yasmin said, fighting to swallow her fear.

Jackal looked up at the ceiling's LiveFotos.

'Well, as pretty as I am,' he said, 'I'm not here so you can take my picture. You need to come with me.'

'Why?' Yasmin asked.

Jackal's barking laugh was as unpleasant as steel chair legs scraped across a concrete floor. 'Why? Because I say so.' He turned and nodded to one of his men.

There was an almighty crash as an officer tipped a shelf of porcelain Sphinxes into a glass display case of jewellery.

Yasmin gasped and Mahmoud jumped to his feet.

'Now look what you made us do,' Jackal sneered.

'Hey, you can't do tha—' Mahmoud shouted.

One of the cops silenced him with a punch to the stomach. Yasmin's brother let out a gasping oomph as he doubled over in pain.

'Don't hurt him!' Yasmin yelled.

Their parents had always told them that if there was a robbery they should give the criminals whatever they asked for and wait until they were gone before calling the police. They never said what to do if the criminals *were* the police.

'The cash register's right there,' Yasmin said desperately. 'Just take the money and go, please.'

'I'm not here for a few thousand pounds,' Jackal scoffed. 'I'm here for *you*, "DARE Award winner" Yasmin Adib. I know how much *you're* worth.'

Yasmin reeled. Her head spun. She felt like she might throw up. This was crazy! She didn't receive her million dollars until she'd spent her week with Felix and the other DARE winners aboard the *Infinite Horizon*. She had to convince Jackal he'd made a mistake.

'I don't have the money yet,' she said. 'If you don't believe me, check any news article about the awards.'

Jackal lifted his mirrored sunglasses and stared at her with eyes so black and cold they might have belonged to a shark. 'I know that,' he spat. 'But I also know how much you're worth to Felix Scott. How much would he pay to make sure one of his precious little winners doesn't get hurt? So you're going to come with me and—'

'She's not going *anywhere* with you!'

Jackal's eyes widened as Radha came into the shop from the hallway. Yasmin had to blink to make sure she wasn't seeing things. Her grandmother had a little silver pistol aimed at the detective's chest.

'Don't shoot!' Jackal begged, lip trembling theatrically. 'Please!' A grin spread across his face as he raised his hands in mock surrender. 'Please, old woman, don't shoot me with that . . . toy.'

Jackal's henchmen burst out laughing. Radha cackled right along with them.

Bang!

Towering on a cliff edge in the Santa Monica Mountains, the Griffith Observatory was crowned by three huge bronze domes, each housing a massive telescope which pointed at the night sky.

Andy and Dylan stopped to catch their breath after rushing into the building, where the crowds were thinning as closing time drew near.

'Phew, we made it,' said Andy.

'Yes!' Dylan's loud response earned him a stormy look from a guard in the foyer.

'The observatory closes in ten minutes,' the uniformed man barked. 'Got that, you two?'

'Yes, sir,' Andy said respectfully. He turned to Dylan, whispering. 'Chill, OK? These are stake-out conditions. We don't want any more unwanted attention from our friends in security ... or any bad guys.'

Maintaining a casual air, Andy waited for the guard to turn his attention elsewhere. Then they crossed to the leather visitor's couch, right where Ethan had said it would be. Andy slid the yellow envelope from his jacket and tucked it between the cushions. Drifting away, hearts hammering, the boys pretended to be engrossed in the swinging pendulums and sparks of lightning shooting from the Tesla coil. But their eyes were actually focused on their InfiniFones, which they'd folded into neat squares in their hands. Each screen streamed footage of the view behind them from tiny FoneDrone cameras docked on the brims of the baseball caps they wore backwards.

'I can't believe I'm doing this,' Dylan said in a shaky voice. 'Aren't you nervous?'

Andy held up his free hand. It trembled ever so slightly. 'I love the adrenalin rush,' he said.

'And your dad doesn't mind?' Dylan asked. 'That is *awesome*. If my parents knew I was doing this, they'd chuck a wobbly.'

He smiled at Andy's confused expression. '"Chuck a wobbly",' he said, 'means "freak out".'

Andy grabbed his arm and nodded at the observatory entrance. Two men had just walked in. Both wore black leather jackets and blue jeans. One guy was bald and chubby, the other man had a bushy beard and long skinny legs. The security guard approached them. 'Sorry, gentlemen, we're closing up in five minutes.'

'We won't need that long,' said Bald Guy as he and Beard Dude brushed straight past.

'Those guys don't look like they're here for a science lesson. It's got to be them,' whispered Dylan.

Andy gave a little nod. Bald Guy and Beard Dude were walking straight for the couch!

Dylan saw that these were two very confident bad guys. They didn't seem at all afraid of getting caught. Instead, Bald Guy stood by the couch while Beard Dude openly ran his hands down between the cushions.

'Score!' he said, pulling out the envelope.

Bald Guy grinned. 'Let me see.'

They huddled together. There was a flash of green when Beard Dude opened the envelope. 'Yep,' he said, tucking it into his jacket. 'This is almost too easy.'

'Five down, two more to go,' Bald Guy said. 'So, where to next?'

Beard Dude whipped out a phone and tapped at its screen. 'Got it!' he said, grinning. 'Looks like we're heading to the dead centre of town.'

Bald Guy looked puzzled.

'Come on,' said Beard Dude. 'You'll see.'

With that, the men hustled to the exit and were gone.

Andy whirled. 'Five down and two to go? This is bigger than just Ethan.'

Dylan nodded, eyes wide behind his glasses. 'Mate, they must be ripping off heaps of kids!'

'I think I know where they're heading,' Andy said. 'Let's go!'

Yasmin's heart thumped as the statue by Jackal's ear exploded and sprayed him with plaster fragments. The shot echoed through the store. Gun smoke drifted to the ceiling. Jackal's mouth fell open in shock. He touched his fingers to his cheek. They came away bloody. He'd been cut by a flying shard.

'Next bullet goes between your eyes,' Radha said, her voice eerily calm. 'Yasmin, Mahmoud, get behind me.'

They scrambled to do what she said.

Jackal snarled. 'I'm going to—'

'Leave!' Radha shouted determinedly. 'You're going to leave and not come back.'

Jackal and his henchmen traded looks. Radha's eyes narrowed.

'Five more bullets left,' she said, the pistol tight in her steady old hand. 'That's one for each of you.'

The detective's eyes flickered. He started reaching inside his jacket. Around the shop, the cops were going for their holstered pistols.

'Grandmother!' Yasmin hissed.

'I see them!' Radha retorted. Her eyes never left Jackal. 'You and your heroes are going to shoot an old woman and two kids?' she said mockingly. 'In a family store? Even a dog like *you* won't get away with that.'

Doubt clouded Jackal's expression.

Radha stepped forward, pistol aimed steadily, grand-children gathered behind her. 'Get out of here, you son of a shoe,' she said, using her worst insult.

Jackal and Radha locked eyes for a long moment. Yasmin could barely breathe with the tension in the air.

'Let's go,' Jackal said finally to his gang of crooked cops, moving slowly away, eyes still on Radha.

The men backed towards the shop's door and slipped out onto the street.

Jackal hovered at the entrance, glaring at Yasmin, Radha and Mahmoud. 'This isn't over.'

'Turn the sign to "Open" on your way out,' Radha said. She waved the gun and Jackal obeyed, flicking the sign over so violently it banged against the glass.

'I'll see you soon, Yasmin,' he said, before disappearing into the bustle outside.

The boys crouched beside a side entrance to Hollywood Forever Cemetery. They'd taken an AutoTaxi from the observatory and arrived at Los Angeles' most famous celebrity graveyard just in time to see Bald Guy and Beard Dude slip through the service gate that someone must have left unlocked for them.

'Dude, this place creeps me out,' Andy admitted under his breath.

Dylan shook his head. 'Staking out the observatory is one thing, but creeping into a graveyard at night?'

'If this is the way we get the scoop then it's what we have to do,' replied Andy, trying to sound brave. 'Come on.'

Dylan inhaled deeply and followed his friend through the side gate.

They walked carefully, slow and quiet, as they prowled the rows of graves, scanning the gloom for a sign of Bald Guy and Beard Dude. Rustling noises seemed to chase them between the tombstones and they stopped every few steps to check they weren't being followed.

An unearthly cry pierced the gloom.

'What's that?' hissed Dylan. It sounded not of this world, like some supernatural creature.

Ahead of them, a bush rustled. The boys tensed.

A peacock strutted into the moonlight.

'It's just a bird,' said Andy, voice quaking. 'Don't be such a scaredy—'

He jumped back, almost knocking Dylan into a monument to Toto from *The Wizard of Oz*.

'What?' Dylan hissed.

'That statue,' Andy said, pointing ahead with a shaking hand at a sculpture of a dead rock star. 'I thought it moved!'

'Just a trick of the shadows and the moon,' Dylan reassured them both. 'We need to chill.'

'Agreed,' Andy said. 'It's not like vampires or werewolves are real.'

'Vampires, werewolves—you had to say that?' Dylan replied with a gulp.

'Let's just worry about the human bad guys,' Andy whispered, eyes flitting around the headstones and crypts, 'who could be anywhere . . . lying in wait.'

'Not helping, mate,' Dylan said in a small voice.

'Come on,' Andy urged. 'We gotta do this.'

The boys crept forward again. Shadows played over marble monuments and in the eerie stillness even the soft crunches of their footsteps seemed to echo around the graveyard.

A laugh—definitely human—made both boys duck. Heart pounding, Andy peeked around a headstone.

'Is it them?' murmured Dylan.

Andy nodded and crouched tighter, Dylan huddled close beside him. They glanced cautiously around the dusty granite grave marker. Bald Guy and Beard Dude were mucking around at the base of a tombstone topped by a massive marble angel. Beardie posed in the same prayerful position as the statue, while Baldie snapped a photo. Both laughed as they checked the result on the screen.

'These guys are hardcore,' muttered Andy. 'They don't seem freaked out by the cemetery at all.'

Andy snuck forward, hoping to get into a better position so he could film them on his InfiniFone.

Before he could line up the shot, Bald Guy turned and seemed to look right at them! 'Hey,' he said. 'Quit goofing off. I thought I heard something.'

Beard Dude looked around as the boys tried to melt into the shadows at the base of the headstone.

'Nah,' the crim said after a minute. 'You're imagining things. There's no-one here. But let's get on with it. I don't fancy being busted in here.'

As Andy and Dylan peered around from their hiding spot, the men checked the vases of a few graves.

'Aha!' Beard Dude said, standing up with an envelope.

His partner moved in. They checked the contents, the boys seeing something green in the low light, and traded fist bumps.

Suddenly, the men were cutting across the rows of stone markers.

'They're headed our way,' hissed Dylan. 'Hide!'

But as he scurried to take cover, his shoulder nudged a pedestal holding the plaster bust of a famous actor. Time seemed to slow as it teetered and then . . .

Ker-rrash!

Wide-eyed, Dylan looked from the shattered statue to Andy's horrified face. 'Sorry,' he mouthed.

But it was too late.

'There *is* someone here!' Beard Dude said. 'They just smashed something over there!'

The boys looked at each other in panic. Footsteps crunched across the pebble path.

'Go?' whispered Dylan.

Andy nodded.

Together, they sprang up.

'Hey!' Beard Dude shouted. 'What're you doing?'

Andy and Dylan ran for it. Legs pumping, they bolted past gravestones and palm trees. When they risked a look over their shoulders, they saw the two men racing up the footpath after them.

'We've gotta lose them!' Andy swerved away, rushing low along a row of headstones. Dylan ran doubled over behind him.

They could hear footsteps crunching relentlessly towards them. None of the monuments provided much cover now the bad guys knew they were there.

But when Andy saw a mini earthmover next to a taped-off area, he had an idea so crazy it might just work.

'Follow me,' he panted. 'Do what I do.'

Keeping low, they ran towards the machine. Ahead of them, a rectangle of tape stuck to plastic poles surrounded a freshly dug grave that yawned like a black hole.

'In!' Andy said, ducking under the tape and dropping into the darkness.

A second later, Dylan landed beside him in the soft ground. 'This,' he hissed disbelieving, '*this* was your plan?'

'*Ssssh!*'

The sky overhead was a moonlit rectangle. Worms wriggled and tumbled from the cut dirt walls. Dylan had never been so scared in his life. He had just followed his friend into an open grave! They'd done most of the work for the bad guys. All they had to do was crank up that earthmover and pile dirt on top of them. He couldn't believe he might shortly be buried alive.

'I've got these if we need them,' Andy whispered, pulling two black bars connected by a length of silver chain from his backpack. 'Nunchaku.'

'You know how to use them?' Dylan asked.

Andy nodded. 'Me and Dad do loads of martial arts.'

Dylan was about to question if they'd be any good for digging their way out of the grave, when they heard footsteps coming closer across the gravel path above.

'Check that out,' one of the men said, close enough that they could hear his raspy breathing. 'It's an open grave.'

Dylan ducked down, making himself as small as he could, while Andy tensed, nunchaku at the ready.

Yasmin and Mahmoud pulled down the security shutter and locked it tight. Trembling, Radha set the silver pistol on the glass counter and sank into a seat.

'Where on earth did you get that gun?' Mahmoud asked.

'Your grandfather won it in a poker game years ago. I didn't even know it was loaded.'

'Are you saying you didn't mean to fire at him?' Yasmin asked incredulously.

Radha shook her head. 'I was so nervous. It just went off accidentally.'

'But what about the whole "five bullets" thing?' Mahmoud asked.

Radha shrugged. 'It's a line from my favourite action movie,' she said mischievously.

Yasmin and Mahmoud looked at each other and then burst out laughing.

Their laughter was cut short by a *thunk-thunk* against the shutter door.

'Someone's there!' Mahmoud said. 'Are they back?'

Radha reached for her weapon.

'Wait!' Yasmin urged. 'Listen.'

'What's going on?' a man demanded.

They sighed with relief—the voice outside belonged to Mr Adib.

'It's Mum and Dad,' Yasmin said. She ran to the shutter and unlocked it.

'Locked up during business hours?' Mr Adib enquired, pushing through the door with colourfully wrapped presents held in his big arms. 'What is the big idea?'

Mrs Adib's worried frown deepened when she stepped inside and saw the broken plaster and shattered jewellery display. 'What in the world happened?'

With the shutter locked tight, the family gathered at the kitchen table. Yasmin, Mahmoud and Radha took turns to explain as Mr and Mrs Adib listened in disbelief.

'I I I ' Yasmin's father said, face red with anger. 'This is an outrage!'

Mrs Adib nodded. 'And what *you* did, Radha, was the silliest—and *bravest*—thing since Cleopatra had a nap with a snake. But—thank you for keeping them safe.'

The women hugged, teary-eyed.

Yasmin felt a tug of guilt. 'If I hadn't entered the DARE Awards, none of this would've happened,' she said softly.

'Nonsense,' Mr Adib said. 'You must not blame yourself.'

'We have to call the police,' Mrs Adib said.

Mr Adib stroked his beard thoughtfully. 'Jackal *is* the police. He might have protection higher up. It could make things worse.'

'He said he would be back,' Yasmin said fearfully. 'We have to do something!'

'I will call my brothers,' her mother said decisively. '*No-one* gets through them.'

Yasmin had three uncles. All of them were huge and had served in the army. Once they were here, the shop would certainly be safe.

'Good idea,' Mr Adib said, clapping his hands.

Yasmin's heart fell at the idea of leaving when her family and the shop were threatened. She wondered if she should call Miss Chen and ask for her SpaceSkimmer flight to Athens to be delayed until she was sure things would be all right.

'We will be fine,' her father said with a smile, as if reading her mind. 'Besides, if they dare come back, we have your pistol-packing grandmother to take care of us.'

Radha chortled.

'Now, we must not let this spoil your big day.'

Mrs Adib nodded. 'Time to open your present!'

Yasmin tore open the wrapping paper to reveal an expensive new backpack. 'Red, white and black!' she said. 'Very stylish and very patriotic. I love it. *Shukran!*'

'No, thank *you*,' her mother said. 'For being the best daughter parents could hope for. We're so proud.'

Mrs Adib nodded at the other gift on the kitchen counter. 'And this is for the best son in the world.'

Mahmoud's eyes widened. 'For me? Really?'

Yasmin's parents nodded. He ripped the paper open and unfolded a red leather motorbike jacket wrapped around a yellow helmet. He tried it on and checked himself out.

'These are awesome, thank you!'

'Well, they're a present for us, too,' Mrs Adib said with a

laugh. 'You know how we worry about the way you ride.'

Mahmoud nodded and hugged his parents.

Yasmin was glad her brother was happy. He had been so supportive of her and genuinely glad when she'd won a DARE Award. She hoped that his wish to be a movie stuntman paid off one day—and that she might even be able to help him realise that dream somehow.

Comforted by the thought of her uncles coming, and warmed by the gifts from her parents, Yasmin began to wonder if the rest of the DARE seven were OK. If Jackal wanted to kidnap her for ransom, she hoped crooks in other countries hadn't gotten similar ideas about her friends. Who knew what sort of creeps might be drawn out of the woodwork by their fame and fortune?

The footsteps got closer and closer.

Dylan started to wriggle and twitch, eyes bulging.

'Stop it!' mouthed Andy.

Dylan grabbed the centipede that had tumbled into his shirt and flung it away.

Crunch.

The sound of a foot on the gravel right near where they were concealed made both boys tense. They held their breath, and balled themselves tight in the blackest shadows against the bottom of the grave wall.

Crunch. Crunch.

There was the flapping sound of tape being lifted.

Crunch. Crunch.

'You'd have to be out of your mind to hide in there,' said one of the men.

Then the moonlight was blotted out, plunging the grave into total darkness, as the men stood right above them. Andy and Dylan didn't dare look up.

'Can't see a thing,' the other guy said. 'Yeah, they must have gone the other way.'

With a kick, he sent a spray of earth and grass down into the grave. Andy and Dylan gritted their teeth but stayed still and silent as they were showered with dirt and worms.

'We should get out of here,' the first guy replied.

Crunch. Crunch. Flap. Flap.

The footsteps moved away.

'I'm gonna phone this in. Just in case someone saw us.'

The men's voices sounded farther away. The boys let themselves breathe. They brushed dirt and worms out of their hair and off their clothes and stood slowly. Andy motioned for Dylan to give him a boost. Standing on his friend's cupped hands, he peeked above the edge of the grave.

At the end of the row of headstones, Beard Dude was looking at his phone. 'We've got one more place to be,' he said to Baldie. 'Let's go. We can make that call on the way.'

Andy dropped back into the grave beside Dylan.

'We're safe for now,' he said. 'But if they're calling their boss about us, we mightn't be for long.'

Dylan shook, barely able to believe that they hadn't been discovered. 'Reckon we've got enough evidence for your dad? And to help your mate Ethan?'

Andy nodded. 'We definitely don't want to keep following them. The sooner they're behind bars the better.'

Once they were sure the men were gone, the boys climbed out of the grave that had saved them and ran as fast as they could to the nearest AutoTaxi.

Back at Andy's place, the boys calmed their nerves with some pizza and built up a theory about what was going on.

The men had completed seven pick-ups just that day. That could mean that dozens or even hundreds of kids were being blackmailed. The fact that they seemed to be getting directions to each location via phone pointed to them being minions of some unseen criminal mastermind.

'Are you sure you want to run the story?' asked Dylan. 'These guys might have some heavy connections.'

'We've gotta stop them,' said Andy. 'My mum always said you have to go after the truth, no matter what. And that's what I'm going to do.'

'OK then. Let's get this story up on *Scoop*!' Dylan said.

With a few verbal commands, the boys uploaded the video of Ethan and the footage from the observatory to the HoloSpace to edit and add a voice-over.

'In just one day, these two criminals could've ripped off up to seven thousand dollars from terrified schoolkids,' Andy narrated. 'That could add up to millions of dollars every year. This *Scoop* exclusive is the first step to stopping them. All the evidence you've seen is being forwarded to the Los Angeles Police Department.'

'Mate, this story's a cracker,' Dylan said when Andy had finished. 'I'd hate to be those two now.'

'Let's hope Dad can make them give up the mastermind,' Andy said. 'So, as co-Scooper, you wanna do the honours?'

Dylan nodded, instinctively wiping pizza grease off his fingers before he pressed the virtual 'Publish' tile floating in front of his face.

'It's live,' he grinned.

'Compose email to the Old Man,' Andy said. The HoloSpace showed a picture of the big cop who'd been so proud of his son at the DARE Awards. 'Upload all files from folder "Grade Scam".' In a flash, the video they'd recorded of Ethan, Bald Guy and Beard Dude attached to the email. 'Send,' Andy said. He looked at Dylan and grinned. 'Let's call Ethan and give him the good news.'

Andy selected Ethan's number. He frowned as his call connected to an automated message. 'The number you have dialled is not in service. Please check the number before calling again.' He was sure it wasn't the wrong number.

'I don't think it's connected,' Andy said, eyes serious. 'I hope he's OK.'

'Maybe he got a new phone?' Dylan said. 'You know, as a precaution?'

Andy let out a whistle. All thoughts of Ethan disappeared as he looked at a graph of *Scoop* traffic on his HoloSpace. It was skyrocketing.

'Wow,' Andy said. 'Look what's boosted traffic to the site.' He pulled a tweet over into the centre of the display.

> **@RealFelixScott**
>
> Congrats @Scoop_AndyF on another important story exposing bad guys and evil deeds in LA. #dreamactrealiseeverything

'Thank you very much @RealFelixScott,' Andy grinned. 'He posted that to his fifty million followers. It's already been re-tweeted heaps of times.'

The boys high-fived.

Like the other winners, Zander had become a minor celebrity after the DARE Awards.

Getting used to his fame was taking some time, and while Zander was happy to be interviewed by the Greek media, he was amused by some of the stranger requests that he got. A television quiz show wanted him to be a contestant. He was asked to be a commentator at a fashion parade. The producers of a popular cooking show wondered if he'd like to be a guest judge.

With no desire to become a famous person who popped up everywhere, Zander politely said no to all of these offers. But there was one invitation that he hadn't been able to resist: to appear at his old primary school's special end-of-year presentation day.

Now, looking very grown-up in a black suit and grey shirt, Zander commanded the stage in St Theodore's hall. With hundreds of students hanging on his every word, he felt like a young version of Felix Scott.

'So, in conclusion,' he said, 'vision, hard work and personal integrity are what the DARE Awards are all about. Thank you for having me back here to speak to you today.'

The students clapped and cheered. Mr Markos, still principal after all these years, bounded onto the stage to shake Zander's hand.

'We're so proud of you,' Mr Markos said. 'We're very grateful to you for taking the time to visit, especially as we understand you're going overseas soon.'

Zander nodded. 'Yes, in a few days I go to Seoul and Sydney to meet up with other DARE Award winners. We all then board the *Infinite Horizon*. From there, I am not sure. But Felix is certain to make it a great adventure.'

Mr Markos smiled. 'Before you leave, there are a few questions from the students.'

Almost every hand in the hall reached for the ceiling. Zander pointed to a boy in the front row.

'Was it hard to make your *NEO Avenger* app?' he asked.

'Like anything,' Zander said, 'it was one percent inspiration followed by ninety-nine percent perspiration. That is to say, anything worthwhile is always a lot of hard work.'

He pointed to a girl at the back.

'Did you know that Felix was behind the DARE Awards?'

Zander allowed himself a little smile. 'I was not sure. I had read his autobiography and knew his motto was "Dream, Act, Realise Everything". So I thought DARE *could* be an acronym and that he *might* be involved. Turned out I was right.'

Zander chose a girl with long pigtails.

'What was it like meeting Felix Scott?' she asked dreamily.

'Because he started out as a young programmer, he is a real inspiration for me,' Zander said. 'I hope to learn as much as I can from him in the time we have together.'

A serious-looking older boy caught Zander's eye. The student stood up and cleared his throat. 'Do you think the DARE Awards were rigged?'

A ripple went through the students. Zander stiffened. 'Rigged?'

'Now,' said Mr Markos into the microphone, 'there's no need for rudeness!'

But the student wasn't done.

'Well,' the boy continued, 'there are seven of you from seven continents, right? But there's hardly any kids in Antarctica, so was Mila included because of Infinity's interests there? And do you think Dylan won just because his parents are famous?'

Zander paused—it was a powerful public-speaking trick he had observed Felix use in New York. The boy blinked, growing uncomfortable in the silence.

'I can understand why you might think that,' Zander said. 'But I assure you, Mila and Dylan won their places on their own merits. From what I understand, she has a formidable grasp of astronomy and he knows more about marine biology than most professors of the science.' Zander smiled at the boy. 'Maybe you should ease up reading so many conspiracy theories?'

The students roared with laughter and the now red-faced student sank back into his seat.

'All right, all right, calm down everyone,' Mr Markos ordered. 'That's all the time we have. Please thank Zander Demeter for being here!'

Zander rode his motor scooter back home through the smoggy streets of Athens. As always, he was grateful to reach the coast road that led to the seaside suburb of Varkiza that he and his grandfather called home. Arriving at the imposing three-storey house set into a hillside, Zander revved up the driveway and came to a stop in the garage.

'*Kalispera!*' called out his white-haired grandfather, George, from the balcony.

'Hello yourself,' Zander yelled back.

In the kitchen, Zander poured himself a glass of water and strolled out onto the balcony.

'How did it go?' George asked, setting his newspaper down on the table.

'As well as I could have hoped,' Zander replied, taking his usual seat opposite.

'I'm glad you had a triumphant return to your school,' George said, raising his glass of juice. '*Yamas!*'

'Yes—cheers!' They clinked glasses. Zander grinned. 'Mr Markos introduced me as St Theodore's most successful former student.'

'Don't get too impressed with yourself,' George chuckled, wagging his finger. 'Never forget, Alexandros, that I changed your nappies!'

Zander laughed. His grandfather was the only person he didn't mind making fun of him—or using his full name—because they had been through so much together. As much as Felix fascinated him, Zander reserved his real respect for his beloved George.

'Have you seen this?' George picked up his newspaper to show Zander a headline.

FELIX SCOTT WILL 'DESTROY THE SOUTH POLE'

Beneath the headline was a picture of Felix Scott next to a hologram projection of one of his proposed research resorts in Antarctica.

'It seems even great people have their critics,' George said. 'This article says his plans could ruin the environment and even threaten the South Pole Peace Talks.'

Zander brought up another article on his phone, this one praising Felix Scott as Environmentalist of the Year, and handed it to his grandfather.

'Who knows what to believe? According to this article, what Felix has planned could actually avoid war and preserve the environment.'

George shrugged. 'Life is complicated when you want to save the world *and* make money.' He closed the window on the phone then stared at the screen. 'What's this?'

'A text message.' Zander frowned. 'From an unknown number.'

'You know what it is?' George asked.

Zander's eyebrows arched. He could tell from his grandfather's tone that he was about to be told.

'This,' George said, tapping the screen, 'is an old symbol that represents the thunderbolts Zeus hurled from the heavens. He used it to defeat his enemies and defend his loved ones. Don't you remember? From the mythology books I used to read to you?'

'I seem to recall something like that,' Zander said.

'Sure, you do,' George mocked gently, 'no time for books with your face stuck in your too-smart glasses and phone all the time. Why does someone send you a Zeus symbol and some random number?'

Zander shrugged. 'My guess is it's Andy,' he offered.

'The American?'

'He called me Zeus at the DARE Awards,' Zander said.

George chuckled. 'It is not an insult to be compared to the king of the gods.'

Zander smiled and turned to soak up the sun. The salty air and the sound of the seabirds calling to each other as they rode the ocean breezes were restful. But for Zander the spectacular location was haunted by a feeling of sadness. After his parents died in a terrible fire that ripped through their computer company's offices, it had been insurance money that paid for this seaside house. In the three years since the tragedy, his grandfather had raised Zander as best he could. Despite his endless teasing, George took huge pride in what his grandson had achieved with his *NEO Avenger* game and the DARE Awards.

'What time does this Egyptian girl arrive?' George asked, changing the subject.

'At seven,' Zander said. 'It's a *very* quick flight from Cairo on a SpaceSkimmer.'

'You're going to meet her at the airport?'

'Of course.'

George took a sip of his juice. 'I saw this Yasmin girl looking at you in New York,' he said with a cheeky grin. 'I think she—'

'Don't say it,' Zander warned.

George chortled. 'I think she likes you.'

Zander felt colour rise in his cheeks. 'I like her, too. But Yasmin and I are only going to be friends. Do you know what you're always going to be?'

His grandfather shook his head.

'A troublemaker.'

George grinned. 'Like grandfather, like grandson, eh?'

'It must be awesomely cool, having movie stars for parents,' Andy said from his bed in the dark.

Dylan sighed in his sleeping bag on the inflatable mattress. 'Depends on your definition of "awesomely cool",' he said.

'What do you mean?' Andy asked.

'I know I'm lucky,' Dylan said. 'They rescued me from a Haiti orphanage. I owe them everything, but ...'

'But?' Andy prompted.

'I spent more time with nannies, minders and tutors than I ever did with them. Whenever we'd go anywhere, it was with a whole entourage of their "people". I felt, I dunno, like a member of their staff. We'd come in on a private plane, take limos to a trendy hotel, have to spend all our time on movie sets or at parties or at the mansions of whoever they were friends with that week.'

Andy chuckled. 'Sounds like hell.'

Dylan smiled wryly. 'I know, I know, I sound like a spoiled brat,' he said. 'But starting boarding school in Sydney was the happiest day of my life.'

'For real?'

'Mate, it was the first time I made actual friends. I got to go on beach camp—that's how I learned to scuba dive and how I decided to be a marine biologist. I mean, I still see

KitKat every few months, and they're good people, but I'm glad I don't have to live with them all the time.'

Andy whistled. 'Dude, that is way harsh. I guess I'm glad I don't know how that feels.' He was quiet for a moment. 'I'd give anything for more time with . . .'

'Your mum?' Dylan prompted.

'Yeah.'

'What happened to her?'

Andy shifted in his bed. 'She was on assignment in Pakistan when that big earthquake hit two years ago. The building she was in collapsed.'

Dylan remembered the news reports about the disaster. 'Mate, I'm sorry.'

'Thanks. I guess I set up *Scoop* as a tribute. You know, carrying on her legacy or whatever. I wanted it to be something she would've been proud of.'

'Well,' said Dylan, 'I'm sure she would be. Especially after today.'

'Thanks, man,' Andy said, and then promptly fell out of bed as the room's sound system let out a sound like a trumpet blast. A video tile with the words 'Yasmin—Accept Call?' appeared in the HoloSpace.

'Accept,' Andy said, standing and turning on the light.

Yasmin materialised in crisp 3D from her bedroom in Cairo. 'Sorry to call so late,' she said. 'I just had to make sure you were all right after watching your *Scoop* story!'

The boys told her they were fine—and not to worry about the time.

Another trumpet sounded and Isabel and Mila's smiling faces appeared from Bogotá. They were sitting in a bedroom where a clock on the wall displayed the local time in Colombia as 3:30 am.

'You guys are up late,' Andy said.

'Yes—or, rather, early,' Isabel corrected, her hair flaring like a pink halo in the glow of her bedroom lamp. 'We're doing an all-nighter. I'm going to show Mila the best dawn view of Bogotá. But we just watched your story on *Scoop*. Wild stuff. You're real action men!'

Beside her, Mila nodded shyly.

'Hey,' Andy said, brushing imaginary lint off his shoulder, 'ain't no thing.'

'Mila,' Dylan said, 'as our future astronaut, how'd you like the SpaceSkimmer flight to Colombia?'

The colour rose in her pale cheeks. 'Oh, yes. Very good.'

'Very good?' Andy said. 'Dylan rated it as "fully sick"—apparently that means, like, awesome times radical.'

Mila's emerald eyes flickered. 'I give it, er, one hundred points out of ten, yes?'

The Chilean girl smiled when her joke brought laughter from the others.

'It sounds incredible,' Isabel said.

Two more trumpet blasts announced JJ and Zander. Both boys joined the call on their SmartGlasses.

'That *Scoop* video was impressive,' Zander said, sitting in a bedroom stuffed with tech gear and exercise equipment. 'Have they caught those two men yet?'

'Not yet,' Andy said. 'But my dad's on the case.'

JJ chuckled in his Seoul bedroom, the window behind him showing distant skyscrapers towering against an autumn afternoon. 'Bad guys and online scammers,' he said. 'Dylan, you're going to be safer when you get to my place in Seoul—and I live fifty kilometres from the world's most dangerous border!'

They all laughed.

'Actually, I'm glad everyone's on this call,' Isabel said, 'because Mila and I have been talking and are wondering— can anyone help us figure out these strange text messages?'

Isabel flicked her and Mila's symbols into the HoloSpace.

Andy and Dylan exchanged a glance and Yasmin gasped.

'We got symbols and numbers just like that,' Andy said.

 'Here's mine.'

'And mine,' Dylan said.

 Then Yasmin shared hers.

'We do not know who sends them,' Mila said. 'They are coming from an—'

'Unknown number,' Dylan finished for her. 'We thought we'd see what we—'

'What you could find out on the internet,' Isabel interjected, 'only for it to lead you here?'

She swiped the Games Thinker website into the HoloSpace.

> EVENTS FOR YOU AS MIND PEACE
> THE FIRST SIGN
> 04:27:03

'That's right!' Andy said.

'I thought mine could be like an artistic kind of eye,' mused Isabel. 'You know, with the pupil, iris and eyelashes around it? But I've got no idea what the number means.'

'My turn to show and tell,' JJ said, pinging his message into the HoloSpace.

'Mine's just letters,' he said, slicking his hair into place across his forehead. 'And, yup, all I get is the Games Thinker as well.'

'ANE,' Dylan mused.

'Maybe it's an acronym,' proposed Zander. 'Like DARE means "Dream, Act, Realise Everything".'

The others nodded.

'Maybe it stands for "Antarctic Natural Environment"?' Mila said quietly.

'Or ... Ancient Near East,' Yasmin said. They all looked at her. 'It's what my area of the world used to be called.'

'Advanced Neurological Engineering?' JJ offered with a shrug, tapping the metal and plastic leg mecha he was resting casually on his desk. 'It's a robotics term.'

The HoloSpace was filled with frowning faces. None of the guesses had shed any light.

'Zander,' Yasmin said softly, 'did you get a symbol?'

The Greek boy nodded and shared his in the HoloSpace.

'Maybe thunderbolts, you know, lightning,' Zander said. He knew as soon as he mentioned Zeus he'd get wisecracks from Andy. 'Actually, my grandfa—'

'How is that lightning?' Andy interjected, frowning at the symbol. 'Looks more like a plane to me.'

'Yup, sure does,' JJ agreed. 'And what's with the ninety-two?'

'Does anyone know what any of the numbers mean?' Isabel asked.

No-one did.

Still scowling at being cut off, Zander's eyes flicked rapidly behind his SmartGlasses, turning movements into computer commands.

'Hey, Z-man,' Andy said to him. 'You're pretty good with computers, why don't you see if you can trace the Games Thinker web address back to an owner?'

'What do you think I'm doing, shopping online for your Christmas present?' Zander shot back, getting laughs from the others. 'I am a step ahead of you.'

Andy grinned. Zander had gotten the better of him.

'I think mine is hieroglyphics,' Yasmin said. 'Not exact, but a representation. We sell souvenirs with a similar symbol in our shop. It is the name of Khufu. He was the pharaoh who built the Great Pyramid at Giza just near where I live. And perhaps these—' she pointed to the little arrows around her symbol, '—make a pyramid?'

JJ nodded. 'Yup, I see it.'

'But *all* of our symbols have those arrows,' Isabel said.

Yasmin agreed, a little deflated.

'Did everyone get theirs at the same time?' Dylan asked.

A quick check confirmed all the symbols had been received eight and a half hours ago.

'We are the only ones to get these symbols, yes?' Mila piped up.

'Good point,' Isabel said, nodding beside her. 'Everyone get on social media and ask around.'

For the next few minutes, the group posted the question on their various profiles. Responses started flooding in.

'Here's what my crew say,' JJ laughed. 'And I quote— "Huh?", "You cray-cray!", "Say what?". You get the idea.'

'My squad, too,' said Isabel.

No-one else's friends knew anything about the mysterious text symbols, either.

'Then it is just the seven of us who got them?' Yasmin asked.

'Seems that way,' Isabel agreed.

'Then they are from him, yes?'

All eyes turned to Mila. She blushed at being the centre of attention.

'Go on,' Isabel encouraged. 'Him who?'

'Felix,' Mila said softly. 'We seven have him in common only. So, he sets for us a test, we are to figure these out, yes?'

Dylan nodded. 'That actually makes sense.'

'Games Thinker would fit, too,' Zander said. 'Felix's initial success came from thinking up new computer games.'

'Seven symbols,' mused Isabel. 'One for each of the seven of us from seven continents.'

'Fits with his thing for seven,' JJ said, clicking his fingers.

Andy shrugged. 'Dudes, maybe we should just, like, call up Miss Chen and ask to speak to Felix about it?'

Dylan punched his friend on the shoulder playfully. 'Mate, if this is from him, don't ya reckon we should try to solve it first?'

'If you insist,' Andy said with a smile.

'Maybe this will be a treasure hunt,' Mila suggested.

Andy rubbed his hands together. 'Now I dig that idea! Zander, has the web address turned up a pot of gold?'

Zander shook his head. 'The transfer protocols are being

rerouted through anonymous third-party servers in—'

'Dude, how about plain English for those of us who don't speak geek?' Andy asked.

Zander dipped his SmartGlasses to stare at Andy through the HoloSpace. 'OK then, An-dee,' he said, speaking so slowly he made the others start laughing. 'What I am saying is that the website cannot be traced.'

Zander smiled smugly but all he got from Andy was a good-natured laugh. 'Glad there's a sense of humour to go along with that brooding Greek god thing you've got going on!'

Zander went to fire back but Isabel shut him down with a pointed look.

'Boys,' she said loudly. 'Focus, OK? So, we agree this *might* be Felix?'

Everyone nodded.

'And this countdown,' she continued, '*might* be how long we've got to decode the symbols and numbers and work out what "events for you as mind peace" means?'

Again they agreed.

'Maybe the numbers are for the lottery?' Andy blurted, getting a few laughs—and a headshake from Zander. 'I might play them just in case. I'll cut you all in if I win big—well, maybe not you, Z-Man.'

Zander didn't smile. 'Does everything need to be a joke?'

'Dude, lighten up,' Andy said. 'You're really—'

'No, you—'

'So,' Isabel said impatiently over the top of them, 'we've

got an eye and a plane. Does anyone else recognise any of the other symbols?'

'It's not a plane,' Zander said. 'It's Zeus's thunderbolt.'

'What?' Andy laughed.

'My symbol.'

'Zeus? Are you for real? That's too funny.'

'Did you send it?' Zander asked accusingly.

Now all eyes turned to Andy. His eyes bulged with amusement. But he shook his head and raised his hand. 'Scout's honour, it wasn't me.'

'How do you know this is Zeus's symbol?' Isabel asked Zander.

He sighed. 'My grandfather told me. It represents the thunderbolt Zeus used to defeat his enemies.'

They digested the information but couldn't see any meaning behind it.

'OK,' Isabel said. 'So that's another one. Anyone else?'

Mila cleared her throat. 'Dylan, your symbol, it is Castor and Pollux, yes? They are the dual stars—Gemini, the twins, if you believe in astrology.'

Now the others saw it.

'Well done, Mila,' Isabel commended.

'Hate to disappoint you, but I'm an Aries,' Dylan said.

Mila gave a little smile.

'Anyone else?' Isabel asked.

There were headshakes all around. They seemed to have reached a dead end.

'Maybe we were just supposed to find the Games Thinker website,' JJ offered. 'Maybe when the timer runs out the website will tell us more?'

'You are saying we give up already?' Yasmin said.

'Nope,' JJ said with a sigh. 'But the big problem is we don't even know what order these symbols go in.'

With a few eye swipes, he sent two rows of symbols from his SmartGlasses into the HoloSpace.

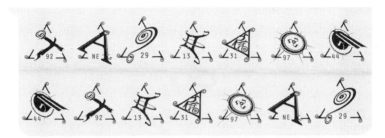

'There are hundreds more combinations like these.'

'Actually, it is five thousand and forty,' Mila said softly. This time she didn't blush. 'I am good at maths.'

They laughed and she smiled shyly.

'So,' Dylan said, running his fingers through his dreadlocks, 'if I'm hearing this right, there's no way we can break this code in the time left?'

'Yup,' JJ said. 'Unless...'

'Unless?' Isabel asked.

'We can find some sort of key,' JJ said.

'I'll let you know if I stumble on one in my bed,' Andy said with a yawn. 'I'm gonna have to bail on this mystery for now.'

Glasses off, Dylan rubbed his eyes. 'It's been a big day.'

'Yes, we must be going soon,' said Isabel. 'If we are to see the sunrise.'

Mila nodded.

JJ laughed. 'I've got somewhere to be, too.' He patted his trendy hair and brushed at his cool shirt. 'But trust me, if anyone's going to crack this puzzle, it's probably going to be a devastatingly handsome dude from Seoul.'

The others laughed.

The DARE winners traded goodnights and good mornings before ending their HoloSpace hook-up.

'All right, let's get some sleep.' Andy yawned. 'We'll hit Laguna Beach tomorrow and see your fishies.'

'OK. Silent.'

'What? Me?'

'No—my phone,' Dylan said. 'I don't want to get woken up because JJ figures out ANE stands for "Audible Nasal Emission".'

Andy guffawed in the darkness.

JJ couldn't believe he was going to be turned into a robot. Not only that, he'd be on display at RoboWorld, Seoul's most popular tourist attraction. Like every South Korean kid, JJ loved the massive theme park on the southern outskirts of the city. He had often been with his parents to ride the roller-coasters, gaze in awe at the massive mecha-machines and giggle at the cheeky androids that joked with the visitors. But this time JJ had been escorted in through the VIP entrance as a special guest. Now he was sitting in a reception room in one of the park's skyscrapers, with a superb view of the floodlit amusements and the Han River beyond shimmering in the pale evening light.

Like the other winners, JJ had done a lot of media since the DARE Awards ceremony. His parents were privacy freaks, but eventually they had let him give interviews on the strict condition that he protect their wishes by not talking about them or revealing where they lived. Not that reporters really wanted to know about his mum and dad anyway. What they wanted to hear was how he'd lost the use of his legs in a car accident when he was two, how at age seven he'd made himself a robo puppy and how he'd always been determined to make leg-mecha so he could leave his wheelchair behind.

But what was *waaay* more exciting than the media

attention was getting a phone call from the owner of RoboWorld. It was a dream come true when Chairman Lee Dae-sung said he wanted a robot version of JJ for his theme park's new RoboFame Hall.

'Chairman Lee is just finishing up a call,' his secretary said. 'Just a few more minutes, please.'

'All good,' JJ said.

JJ used his InfiniFone's mirror app to make sure he looked his best. Nothing stuck in his teeth. Hair still in place across his forehead. His white leather jacket, nano-fibre ColorShift shirt and skinny white jeans hadn't somehow fallen apart since he last checked two minutes ago.

Satisfied, JJ flicked to the Games Thinker website. There were only a few hours left on the countdown. Try though he had, he hadn't been able to crack the code or make sense of 'events for you as mind peace'.

At the very least, JJ was deter-mined to make sense of the letters *he'd* received. He brought up his symbol and stared hard at it.

Maybe it was an acronym. Maybe the NE came first! He clicked his fingers—NEA! That could mean Near Earth Asteroids, which was close to Zander's game *NEO Avenger*, which was all about defending against 'near-Earth objects'. NEA also meant North-East Asia, which was where he lived. But both explanations felt forced.

JJ sighed. The letters could mean almost anything. They could even be a person's initials. What also puzzled him was why he was the only one that had been sent letters and not a symbol with numbers. Or maybe he *had* gotten numbers! A was the first letter of the alphabet so it meant one, while N was fourteenth and E was the fifth. But looking up various combinations of one, fourteen and five online yielded ... nothing.

'Chairman Lee will see you now,' the secretary said. She led JJ on his softly whirring legs into a majestic office. One whole wall was a window with a view straight onto the peak of the TransMecha roller-coaster. Behind soundproof glass, visitors screamed by silently.

A silver-haired man waited in front of a desk the size of a small battleship. His suit was immaculate and JJ worried that he should've dressed up more. But it was too late now.

Chairman Lee bowed slightly. 'Mr Park,' he said formally, using JJ's family name. 'We are most honoured to have you as our guest.'

JJ returned the bow, shook Chairman Lee's hand and gratefully received the man's business card.

As South Korean culture dictated, he studied the card for a careful moment before placing it into his wallet and taking out his own card he'd printed especially for the occasion. All it said was—*Park Jae-joon (aka 'JJ') DARE Awards Winner.*

Chairman Lee nodded and slipped the card inside his suit jacket. The formalities over, he pointed to a couch. JJ sat on the edge of the leather seat.

'We are most proud of your achievement,' the chairman

said, 'and privileged that you have agreed to allow us to make a robot like you.'

'Thank you,' JJ said politely. A smile spread across his face. Despite how he was meant to behave, he couldn't contain his excitement for another second. 'Chairman, I'm *so* excited about this!' he blurted. 'A RoboJJ? It's the best . . . thing . . . ever!'

The older man allowed himself an amused nod. 'You sound like my grandson,' he said. 'Well, Jae-joon, let me show you the lab where your robotic self will be born.'

The chairman led JJ to the elevated moving walkway that whisked them through the glass tunnel network that extended across RoboWorld like a hi-tech spider web. On the avenues below them, kids and parents munched fairy floss as droids from *Galactic Quest* clanked about. Overhead, more park visitors screamed with delight as a roller-coaster corkscrewed around a fire-breathing MechaDragon.

'Programmers, meet Mr Park Jae-joon,' the chairman said when they entered a vast security-controlled lab.

As one, the white-coated men and women stopped what they were doing to bow to the chairman and JJ.

'Hi,' JJ said, returning the gesture, feeling both important and awkward. 'Nice to meet you all.'

'This way,' the chairman said. He led JJ to a large white room fitted with exercise equipment and computer gear.

'Project Jae-joon,' the chairman commanded. 'Activate.'

A circular porthole on the floor opened and a silver

cylinder hummed up into the room. Steel panels opened with a quiet whoosh.

'Whoa!' said JJ when he saw the robot inside. Apart from lifeless eyes, too-smooth skin and hair parted the wrong way, this cyborg was an exact replica of himself. 'That is . . . freaky.'

'Hello,' the RoboJJ said in a monotone version of JJ's voice. 'My name is Jae-joon, also known as JJ.'

JJ smiled. 'Hello, you—I mean, almost-me.'

The chairman nodded. 'Still a work in progress. Ask him a question.'

JJ gulped. What to ask himself? 'Ah,' he said with a nervous laugh, 'what is your—my—favourite food.'

'Data not found,' RoboJJ said, its expression blank. 'My name is Jae-joon, also known as JJ.'

'See,' the chairman said. 'That's why I asked you here. While we used footage from your television interviews to get started, now we need all the personal touches to make him as like you as possible.'

'Deactivate,' the chairman said. 'Return to holding.'

The silver cylinder closed around RoboJJ and slid back beneath the floor.

Shaking off the weird feeling of seeing his double put into storage like a winter coat, JJ listened as the chairman explained the process that would complete RoboJJ.

'We will record everything,' he said, 'facial expressions, speech patterns, body movements and some of your memories and brainwaves. We'll scan your robotic legs and our engineers will manufacture exact duplicates. Once they are fitted, all your data is uploaded into the bio-behaviour software. Then we do some final printing to get the eyes, skin and hair right. When finished, he will be indistinguishable from the real you.'

JJ didn't know what to say—what he'd just seen and heard was totally weird and totally cool. He smiled to himself at the prank possibilities.

'Any questions?' the chairman asked.

'Can he sit my history exam for me tomorrow?' JJ smiled.

His parents had only let him take this meeting with the chairman once he'd agreed to spend his whole day studying for his final school test of the year.

'I am afraid not,' the chairman answered with a grin. 'It will be a few days before he is fully operational. But then, yes, theoretically, he could pass any exam as well as you—or even better.'

'Better?' JJ said, trying not to sound irritated.

The chairman gave a little nod. 'Connected to the internet, he will acquire, store and retrieve information faster than any human.'

'So,' JJ said, 'I won't be able to beat myself at chess?'

'I'm afraid not.'

'Well,' he sniffed, 'I bet I could stump him with knock-knock jokes!'

The chairman surprised JJ with a nod. 'Actually, yes—recreating a sense of humour is the most difficult thing.'

JJ grinned. 'At least I've still got an edge.'

Working quickly, a team of technicians hooked JJ up to dozens of electrodes and placed him in a chamber dotted with hundreds of lasers and cameras. For an hour, JJ walked around the room, jumped on a mini trampoline, jogged and then ran on a treadmill as he was tracked to the micrometre from every angle. Then, for another hour, he had to recite the alphabet, repeat hundreds of words that flashed on a screen and respond to almost as many questions, ranging from 'What's your favourite food?', where he answered 'tacos with the works', to 'What's your biggest fear?', which was 'definitely enclosed dark spaces'.

'We're all done,' the chairman said, stepping into the room as a technician removed the last electrode from JJ's neck. 'A few days from now, Project Jae-joon will look, move, talk and even think like you.'

JJ nodded. 'I can't wait to meet me.'

Chairman Lee offered a bow and extended another card in both hands. JJ took the shiny, black plastic rectangle, which looked like a blank credit card.

'This card guarantees free lifetime entry to RoboWorld for you and your guests,' the chairman said. 'And that includes as much food and drink as you want.'

'Are you *kidding*?'

The chairman smiled and shook his head. 'No kidding.'

'Thank you!' JJ bowed and shook the chairman's hand. 'So I just show this card and I can visit whenever I want, and it's an all-you-can-eat sorta deal?'

Chairman Lee laughed. 'Actually, the card is more of a ceremonial token. We've programmed all of our attractions and cafes to recognise your face. You're part of the RoboWorld family now.'

After leaving the research labs, JJ checked the countdown on his phone.

THE FIRST SIGN
00:29:09

He was running out of time to solve his piece of the puzzle. But now, led by tempting aromas, JJ wasn't thinking about the First Sign—he was following his nose to a fast-food stand.

'Good evening, Jae-joon, also known as JJ,' a robot in a tuxedo said from behind the counter as soon as JJ approached.

JJ grinned—he really would have to speak to the chairman about the whole name thing.

'Would you like the spicy beef taco with cheese, sour cream and guacamole?' the robot asked.

JJ laughed. The questions he'd just answered meant that RoboWorld really did know him now. 'Better make it four,' he said.

Another chef robot expertly assembled the tacos and handed them over, complete with his favourite drink.

Wolfing down his feast, JJ felt like he'd won the DARE Award all over again. He had a golden ticket to his favourite place, not just for a day but for *life*. But JJ realised it'd be a mistake to risk his favourite roller-coaster so soon after stuffing himself. Hurtling around MechaDragon's 'Twists of Terror' now might mean puking up his guts. That wouldn't be a good look for anyone, but especially not for a newly minted member of the RoboWorld family.

JJ needed something gentler. The closest attraction was the RoboFame Hall. Not quite as exciting—but it'd be cool to see where his robo-bro would soon be on display.

With a nod to the uniformed humanoid Guardbot stationed outside, JJ strolled into the RoboFame Hall. The exhibition started right inside the entrance with a man in robes about to hammer an anvil.

'Hi, Jae-joon, also known as JJ,' said the robotic ancient dude as he swung metal on metal with a resounding clang. 'My name is Hephaestus. In Ancient Greek mythology, I was born crippled but I went on to do great things, building robots to serve on Mount Olympus. Would you like to know more?'

Although JJ dug that this dude's backstory was like his own, he wanted to keep moving so he had time for that roller-coaster ride before he went home.

'Not now, thanks, Heph,' he said.

Hephaestus resumed his statue pose. That was the good thing about robots. They didn't take things personally.

Under other spotlights were figures from Indian and

Chinese legends, Leonardo da Vinci's mechanical knight and even automated ducks and foxes from the Middle Ages. It was surprising that robot history stretched back so far.

But what really intrigued JJ was the fake robot from nearly one hundred years ago. It was a huge shiny thing with a head like a silver garbage bin decorated with big cartoon eyes, a triangle nose and ridiculous oversized ears.

'Hi Jae-joon, also known as JJ,' the robot said, detecting his presence. 'My name is Alpha. I was famous in the 1930s when my inventor claimed I was the world's first man-machine. I could supposedly hold conversations, smoke cigars and fire a gun. Would you like to know more?'

JJ laughed. 'Yup.'

'Despite my name, Alpha, which is the beginning of the alphabet in Greek, I wasn't the beginning of the robot age,' it said in a sad voice. 'All of my tricks were done with hidden microphones and wires worked by people offstage. But in the next exhibition room, you will see the true alphas of the robot age.'

But JJ had lost interest in seeing any more displays.

All he could think about was the name of this silly robot in front of him—*Alpha!*

JJ pulled out his phone and looked at the text he'd received.

He *had* been sent a symbol after all! It was an *alpha*! It indicated beginning—and that could mean something when it came to decoding the First Sign!

With fresh eyes, JJ looked at the image on the screen. Perhaps it wasn't ANE but alpha followed by an N and an E.

What was the most common N-E?

'North-east,' JJ whispered to himself. Like a light going on, it was suddenly clear. If he was right, then the numbers below the rest of the symbols could be map coordinates!

JJ jumped up and down, roller-coasters far from his mind. He was sure he'd solved a key part of the puzzle, even if there were still a lot of ways to combine the numbers.

He checked his phone and saw he was almost out of time.

THE FIRST SIGN
00:09:43

JJ desperately wanted to call the others and impress them with his breakthrough. But he also wanted to solve the whole puzzle before time ran out. Ten minutes left. It made sense that alpha came first. Knowing that, he might just crack the code in time!

It had taken hours, but Yasmin was finally packed.

'Got your passport?' her mum asked.

Yasmin tapped the jeans pocket that held her phone and passport.

'All I need now is my journal,' Yasmin said. She'd left it in the rooftop garden that morning. 'I will just be a minute.'

Yasmin bounded up the stairs, her heart pounding. As scary as the confrontation with Jackal had been, she hadn't mentioned her troubles in her conversation with the other DARE winners. The others all seemed to be safe and she didn't want to worry them unnecessarily. Her family had been cleaning up the shop, sweeping up broken merchandise, and Mahmoud had been grumbling about cleaning the paint off the security camera. Her uncles had gone home to their families. Things were returning to normal, and she wanted to put it all out of her mind so she could look forward to her trip to Athens. She brought up the seven mysterious symbols on her phone again, and noticed the clock was still ticking down.

> **THE FIRST SIGN**
> **00:00:29**

Yasmin looked out across the rooftops and at the pyramids rising up against the sand and sky. She nodded as if to say goodbye. Out there everything would be as it usually was on a busy Sunday afternoon. Visitors would be swarmed by touts selling trinkets. Tourists would be riding camels and imagining themselves back in the days of Tutankhamen. Families would be posing for comical selfies in which they 'held' the monuments between their fingers.

She glanced back at her phone.

THE FIRST SIGN
00:00:15

Yasmin laughed nervously. The ticking clock seemed like a premonition, though she didn't know of what. But her smile flatlined when she glanced back at the desert.

Something was wrong. Very wrong.

High above the pyramids a silver object streaked down towards the earth.

A shooting star? Maybe a mirage of some sort?

Yasmin tried to blink it away. But the silver streak didn't disappear. And desert illusions didn't make the sound of rolling thunder that now reached her ears. She squinted.

The streak was a military fighter plane, racing down from the heavens. Its sweptback wings shone while the jet engines roared and left a vapour trail against the blue sky.

Yasmin wondered what was going on. If this was some sort of training exercise, she'd never seen anything like it.

In a heartbeat, terror overtook her—the jet looked like it was on a collision course with the Great Pyramid!

She gasped.

But at the last moment, the plane veered away wildly.

'Oh, thank—' Yasmin started to say.

Except now she saw the plane had fired a missile a second before it swooped clear.

Krrrraaaawhooooosh!

The rocket left a tunnel of smoke in the sky as it hurtled towards the Great Pyramid.

Yasmin told herself she had to be dreaming. That this wasn't happening.

But it was.

'Oh, no,' she whispered helplessly. 'Please, no!'

She screamed as the missile slammed into the peak of the Great Pyramid with a brilliant red-and-white flash. Chunks of stone sprayed as a smoky fireball punched high into the sky. Debris avalanched down the ancient monument's steep slopes. Almost a kilometre away, Yasmin's building shuddered under the impact of the shockwave. Moments later Giza was engulfed by a terrible roar that seemed to swallow up every other sound. Yasmin fell to her knees, sobbing. Spewing fire and smoke, the Great Pyramid looked like a volcano. The explosive howl subsided, replaced by sirens and screams, rising from all around.

Yasmin was dimly aware of a second explosion out near the horizon and saw what looked like a white parachute drifting down to the desert sands.

Yasmin hauled herself to her feet. The peak of Egypt's pride, the famous, heavy stones that had been in place for nearly five thousand years, had been reduced to rubble. But while the damage was terrible, Yasmin knew there would be thousands of tourists and locals around its base and in the path of the falling rocks. 'All those people,' Yasmin whispered. Unable to bear looking upon the devastation any longer, she lowered her gaze. Again, her eyes came to rest on the phone in her hand.

12:56:21

Despite her shock, Yasmin dimly registered that the timer had not just hit zero but had reset and was counting down all over again. She couldn't bring herself to wonder what it could mean.

'What happened?' Mr Adib asked breathlessly, bolting across the roof to her side, stopping by his daughter to take in the sight of the smoking pyramid. 'Are you OK?'

Tears rolling down her cheeks, Yasmin nodded numbly and reached out to grasp her father's arm. 'A p-plane—fired a missile into the pyramid and then crashed in the desert.'

Mahmoud skidded to a stop next to them and gasped. 'Was it an accident?'

Yasmin shook her head. 'I don't think so.'

They stood in shocked silence.

'Look,' her brother said, holding up his phone for Mr Adib to see. 'It's already on the internet.'

The men's eyes filled with tears as they watched footage of the attack uploaded from a tourist's phone. But Yasmin didn't need to relive the horror. She sat heavily, head in her hands, on the edge of the lounge. After a few moments, her mind went back to the mysterious symbols on her phone.

Two symbols now took on a sinister meaning.

'Khufu, plane ... Zeus ... lightning bolt,' she murmured. 'I-I don't believe it ...'

And yet, there it was—the hieroglyph of the pharaoh whose pyramid had just been attacked, beside what Zander had said was a bolt from the heavens!

Yasmin tried to tell herself she was just in shock. There was no way text messages could've predicted the disaster. Surely the timer couldn't have counted down to the attack. It *had* to be a coincidence. It just *wasn't* possible.

But deep in her heart, Yasmin felt the truth. Somehow, the First Sign had pointed to this horrific act.

Yasmin jumped up as black helicopters swooped low over the Giza rooftops and more fighter jets streaked through the sky.

'What's happening?' Mahmoud yelled. 'Is it a war?'

Yasmin thought it was even worse than that. To her this felt like it might be the beginning of the end of the world.

'Everyone, downstairs!' Mr Adib shouted at the top of his lungs. 'Now!'

The Signmaker

Inside the secret headquarters, bathed in a golden glow, the Signmaker leaned forward in an expensive leather seat, totally absorbed in a bank of screens and HoloSpaces. With money and resources virtually unlimited, the Signmaker was surrounded by ultra-modern, limited edition and, in some cases, one-of-a-kind computer and communications technologies. TV news, hacked satellites and surveillance cameras showed smoke billowing from the Great Pyramid and the jet's wreckage burning out in the Egyptian desert. Social media and phone networks were going crazy. The Signmaker smiled. The world was watching, talking, wondering—even if they didn't know why yet—and that was even before they learned that a second disaster was unfolding in another part of Egypt.

With laser-like focus, the Signmaker's attention switched to real-time footage of Giza. Short, sharp voice commands brought up a clear image of Yasmin and her father and brother. Audio came via the family's own smart phones.

'Everyone, downstairs,' Mr Adib barked. 'Now!'

With another voice command, the Signmaker adjusted the satellite image. The Egyptian detective and his men were in place outside Yasmin's family store.

The Signmaker was pleased. The Cairo cop had been

paid to make sure the DARE Award winner was safe. It looked like he was doing his job.

The Signmaker nodded. Everything was going perfectly to plan.

'So, this is Bogotá,' Isabel said. 'What do you think? Worth the trouble?'

The girls had left before dawn to reach La Calera lookout and watch the sun rise. Colombia's striking capital city was also spread out below them as far as the eye could see. It was an almost endless sprawl of buildings, from hillside shanty towns to suburbs of low-rise apartments to shining skyscrapers, all framed by the distant green mountains.

'*Si*,' Mila said, smiling as she stifled a yawn. 'Worth it, yes.'

Keeping awake all night hadn't been their only trouble that morning.

Isabel's neighbourhood adjoined some of the poor shanty towns, or *favelas*, where people sometimes found themselves in the crossfire between police and gangs.

While she had grown used to occasional nights interrupted with shouts and gunshots, she hoped Mila wouldn't have to endure any disturbances during her brief visit. The *favelas* had been quiet overnight, thankfully, but her guest hadn't been entirely spared the pleasure of seeing Colombia's security forces in action. That was because their early-morning taxi had been stopped twice at police checkpoints. As much as Isabel was against the gangs that intimidated her city, President El Cerco's heavy security policy could seem every bit as scary, like a cure that was as bad as the disease.

'Photo?' Mila said now. The girls huddled in the morning chill while she held her phone out to snap them. They admired the selfie.

With her red boots, blue jeans, lime bomber jacket and pink hair, Isabel looked like a punk rainbow in the morning light. She was a total contrast to Mila, whose green eyes were the only spots of colour against her pale face, black short hair, black jumper and skirt. What they had in common were warm smiles for each other.

'Nice,' Isabel said.

Mila nodded. She used her phone to take a photo of Bogotá below them. 'This is so different to my home.'

'You mean the poverty and the soldiers?' Isabel couldn't help being aware that the other DARE Award winners came from wealthier and safer backgrounds than she did.

'True, this is different,' Mila agreed. 'But it is not what I mean. What is to me so amazing is for so many strangers to all live so close together, yes?'

'Eight million,' Isabel said, eyes on Bogotá's sprawl. 'Give or take half a million. No-one really knows for sure.'

'I am living in Antarctica with one hundred and seventy people at Villa Las Estrellas,' Mila said. 'Everyone knows everyone.'

'Villa Las Estrellas,' sighed Isabel. '"Star town"—what a lovely name. No wonder you want to be an astronaut.'

Mila blushed a little. 'It is the dream for me. Not as

important as your dream to build neighbourhood art centres for the children.'

'Ha!' Isabel said. 'Reaching for the stars, what could be bigger than that? Whatever you want, dream big or don't bother—that's my motto!'

Mila laughed and snapped some more photos.

'Hey, it's nearly time,' said Isabel, holding up her phone to show the Games Thinker website as it entered its last sixty seconds.

'One minute,' Mila nodded. 'What do you think is going to happen?'

Isabel shrugged. 'Probably nothing.'

They stood side by side, heads together, and Mila giggled as her friend counted down the seconds like it was New Year's Eve.

'*Tres, dos, uno!*'

THE FIRST SIGN
00:00:00

Nothing happened. And then the timer reset and the words all disappeared.

12:57:00

'Pah!' Isabel said. 'No big solution to the puzzle!'

Mila smiled. 'Maybe we have been given more time to figure it out?'

Isabel shrugged and glanced to where their taxi driver was waiting in the car park. She could hear the soccer game he was listening to on the radio.

'I want to show you my favourite cafe,' she said. 'Feel like some breakfast?'

Mila's stomach rumbled.

'I'll take that as a "yes".'

The girls burst out laughing.

Their cabbie drove them back into the city along the winding mountain road, past apartment buildings and mini malls set into the steep inclines, getting ever more excited by the soccer game on the radio.

'After breakfast we could go to Usaquén,' said Isabel. 'It's this funky little village inside the city centre and there's an awesome market on Sundays. Plenty of stuff to buy and good music to listen to.'

Mila nodded enthusiastically. 'Antarctica has many penguins—but markets not so much.'

Isabel laughed. She liked Mila's quirky sense of humour.

'Defence, defence!' the cabbie said, thumping his hand on the steering wheel. The soccer crowd erupted with a roar as the announcer shouted, 'Goal!'

'Gah!' the driver cried. 'Hopeless.' In disgust at his team, he angrily changed the radio station.

'. . . Great Pyramid in Egypt,' a sombre male voice was saying. 'Witnesses report—and videos confirm—that a military fighter jet fired a missile at the ancient monument before crashing into the desert. At this time there's no confirmation as to the extent of the damage to the structure or loss of life.'

'Oh, no!' Isabel said, face ashen.

'Yasmin—her house,' Mila said softly, eyes glittering, 'is close to there, yes?'

Isabel gulped, pulled out her phone, frantically bringing up Yasmin's number.

Mila looked on, biting her lip. Isabel shook her head. 'Voicemail,' she said. 'Let's not panic. I'll try again in a little while.'

After skirting the edge of Bogotá's glitzy fashion and tech precincts, the cab dropped them off in the historic Candelaria district. Isabel anxiously led Mila along a cobblestone street to Magdalena's, a cafe on the ground floor of an old colonial building. It was noisy with people chattering as they watched the news on wall screens and checked social media on their phones for updates.

Isabel and Mila stood transfixed, horrified by footage of the attack.

'...no death toll has yet been announced,' a news anchor was saying, 'but Sunday is one of the busiest tourist days at the pyramids...'

'Come,' Isabel said, leading Mila to an empty space at a long shared table. It was covered with paper so people could doodle with crayons while they ate. Looking around, Mila saw that the walls of the cafe were decorated with the artwork left behind by customers. Isabel called Yasmin again. She shook her head. 'Still no answer.'

'*Hola*, Isabel,' said a waiter, approaching their table. 'You heard the news? One of your DARE friends is from Egypt, aren't they?'

Isabel nodded.

'Any word on her?'

'Not yet,' Isabel said. 'We're a little worried.'

'I'm sure she's all right,' the waiter said.

'Thanks,' Isabel said. 'By the way, Pablo, this is Mila.'

Pablo gave a little wave. 'Of course. I saw you on TV. Welcome to Bogotá.'

'*Gracias*,' Mila said, colour rising in her cheeks.

The waiter gazed back at the wall screen and shook his head. 'Who would do such a thing?'

'A crazy person, that's who,' Isabel said sternly.

Pablo sighed. 'Too many of them in the world.' He took out his order pad. 'Girls, can I get you anything?'

Isabel looked at Mila. 'OK for me to order?'

Mila nodded.

The waiter jotted down her choices and was reading back the order to Isabel when her phone rang.

'Hi guys,' JJ said, frowning behind SmartGlasses as he checked his phone. 'Have you heard about Egypt?'

'Of course,' Isabel said. 'We're watching it now.'

'We have tried to call Yasmin but it goes to voicemail,' Mila added.

'Me, too,' JJ gulped. 'The news just said three people are

confirmed dead so far but that hundreds more are injured.'

Isabel and Mila glanced at the wall screen, now showing the same update.

JJ nodded. 'I'm going to try to loop in the others.'

He tried calling Andy and Dylan, but their phones both went to voicemail. 'Makes sense,' Isabel said. 'They probably wouldn't be up yet.'

But Zander answered immediately, his image appearing on Isabel's and JJ's screens. He was in his bedroom, amber eyes worried behind SmartGlasses.

'Egypt,' he said simply, 'it is just terrible.'

'Have you spoken to Yasmin?' Isabel asked.

'I could not get through,' he replied.

'That's what we're worried about,' JJ said fretfully.

'The phone networks in Egypt are probably in meltdown because so many people are trying to call,' Zander said. 'We should stay calm.'

'Calm!?' Isabel cried. 'I'm not feeling very calm about this!'

At her side, Mila nodded.

'Yasmin will be safe,' Zander said. 'Think about it. She and her family have lived by the pyramids their whole lives. Why would they go there today?'

Mila's tense shoulders relaxed a little and she looked at Isabel. 'This makes sense, yes?'

'I hope you're right,' Isabel said. 'But I'm still going to freak out until we know for sure that Yasmin's safe.'

JJ clicked his fingers. 'With everything that's happened

in Egypt, I nearly forgot.'

'Forgot what?' Isabel asked.

JJ shrugged. 'Not that it's important now but I think I figured out what my part of the First Sign meant.'

They waited for him to go on.

'OK, so I *did* get a symbol. It's not an "A", it's alpha, the first letter of the Greek alphabet. I think it's meant to symbolise "beginning".'

Zander slapped a hand to his forehead. 'Of course,' he said. 'I should have seen it! But the NE threw me off. Sorry.'

'Not your fault,' JJ said. 'It got past all of us. I also—'

'And it ties in with my Zeus symbol,' Zander cut in.

'What *I* was about to say,' JJ said a little testily, 'was I think the NE stands for north-east. The numbers might be coordinates, you know, longitude and latitude so you can find things on a map.'

'Some silly puzzle doesn't matter now,' Isabel snapped, 'not with Yasmin in danger.'

'Guys!' Everyone fell silent at Mila's raised voice. 'The symbol of the pharaoh who built the pyramids? The Zeus bolt that comes from the sky like the missile from the jet? The First Sign—it is like a . . . prediction?'

All eyes went to Mila.

Beside her, Isabel gasped. 'The countdown! Please don't tell me—'

'Yup,' JJ said, looking up from his phone. 'I just checked. The timer hit zero fifteen minutes ago—right when the pyramid was attacked.'

They were silent for a long, heavy moment.

'No.' Zander shook his head. 'A coincidence—it has to be.'

'I wish it was,' JJ said, eyes wide with fear. 'I've just texted you all something.'

Ringtones echoed as his message was received.

29.9792° N, 31.1344° E

'Are these ... coordinates?' Zander asked.

JJ nodded.

'For where?' Isabel. 'It can't—'

'It is,' JJ said gravely. 'Put the numbers in that order and you get ...'

All eyes were on him. JJ gulped and forced himself to keep speaking.

'You get the longitude and latitude of the Great Pyramid of Giza.'

The television in the Adib family lounge room showed news-chopper footage of Giza's streets, jammed with panicking people and honking cars. As Yasmin and her family watched in horror, the camera zoomed in on men in woollen masks with guns carrying electronic goods from a shattered shopfront.

'Looters,' Mr Adib said in disgust, eyes flicking towards the store's steel shutter. 'Those criminals are using this chaos as an excuse to run rampant.'

Shouts rang loudly from the street just outside the shop. Mr and Mrs Adib hugged Yasmin and Mahmoud tighter to them on the couch, while Radha clutched her worry beads and murmured a prayer.

Now the television flashed to shaky footage of a hand-cuffed man in an air-force jumpsuit being dragged along a desert road by heavily armed soldiers.

Seeing the camera, the terrified pilot screamed a single word before he was bundled into the back of a black van, which immediately roared off in a flurry of dust.

'What did he say?' Mr Adib asked.

'"Offline"' Yasmin said. 'What does that mean?'

'Maybe it *was* an accident,' Mahmoud mused.

The screen now cut to a grey-haired news anchor trying to appear in control. 'As you can see, amateur footage of the pilot's capture has been released,' he said. 'From the uniform, it seems the as-yet-unidentified man who flew the F-16 fighter jet is an Egyptian Air Force officer. Authorities have not yet issued a statement. The question everyone's asking now is whether this was a deliberate attack or the result of a terrible technological malfunction.'

Suddenly, urgent red words flashed across the screen—

• BREAKING STORY—SUEZ CANAL INFERNO! •

—as the news channel showed a new horror almost as hard to believe as the pyramid attack. A super-cargo ship—half a mile long and ten storeys tall—was burning out of control in the narrow Suez Canal. Standing amid reeds on the shore, a safe distance from the unfolding disaster, a female reporter tried to make sense of what was happening.

'About twenty minutes ago, the *Futura*, which is one of the world's largest ships, experienced a catastrophic engine meltdown,' she said. 'A blaze has ripped through the cargo decks with fire-control systems failing.'

Boom! Boom!

The reporter flinched, then whirled around as the camera zoomed in on orange flames flaring from splits along the *Futura*'s massive steel hull.

'What you're hearing and seeing,' she said shakily, 'appear to be explosions originating from the cargo holds. While the crew has evacuated safely, authorities say it's only a matter of time before the ship sinks, blocking the Suez Canal and plunging Egypt deeper into crisis.'

Twenty minutes ago, Yasmin thought.

That meant the *Futura* engine had gone into meltdown just as the jet's missile slammed into the Great Pyramid.

At zero on the countdown!

Yasmin glanced at her phone. She had missed calls from Isabel and Mila and Zander. She knew they'd be worried and she'd call them just as soon as she could. But what made her heart sink was that the phone's screen still showed a countdown on the Games Thinker website.

12:37:13

What was it ticking down to *now*?

Yasmin didn't know. But she knew it could not be anything good.

'I can't believe this,' Isabel whispered in the cafe.

'Neither can I,' said Mila, shivering at her side.

On Isabel's phone screen, Zander's eyes raced back and forth behind his SmartGlasses as he double-checked what JJ had said about the countdown and coordinates. 'You're—you're *right*,' he said, shaking his head. 'This is . . .'

'Insane,' JJ said.

Zander nodded.

No-one spoke for what seemed like the longest time.

Mila held up her phone.

12:35:21

'It resets at zero,' she said in a quaking voice. 'What will happen at the next zero? We must find this out, yes? Yes?'

Snapping out of their shock, the others nodded.

'We have to decode the other symbols,' Zander said. 'The answer has to be there—or in the message, "Events for you as mind peace".'

Isabel shook her head. 'There's certainly no peace of mind in this event!'

'At least with the coordinates, we know the order the symbols go in,' JJ said, swiping at his phone. 'I'm texting them to everyone in order now.'

Numbers = coordinates for Great Pyramid at Giza
29.9792° N, 31.1344° E
Countdown = 00:00 = missile attack

Each of them studied the row of symbols intently.

'So the alpha's at the beginning,' JJ said, 'then we've got that weird spiral thing.'

'Could it be a question mark?' Mila offered.

'Maybe,' Zander said. 'Isabel, if you were right about yours being an eye, then where it is placed has it watching Zeus's lightning bolt hitting Khufu's pyramid.'

'Meaning?' she asked.

Zander shrugged. 'Maybe whoever sent it wants us to be eyewitnesses?'

Mila shivered at the thought. 'But how does the Gemini sign fit in? I don't—'

A gasp went up from Magdalena's customers, echoed by JJ and Zander as their screens relayed the breaking news. Isabel and Mila fell silent as the cafe's TV showed the super-cargo carrier ablaze and sinking in Egypt's Suez Canal.

For the next few seconds no-one spoke as they absorbed the scale of the new calamity.

Mila's eyes widened. 'Gemini,' she murmured.

'What?' Isabel asked distractedly.

'Castor and Pollux,' Mila reminded them. 'The twins. They are born at the same time,' she said. 'Like these two attacks, yes?'

Zander jumped to his feet and paced around his bedroom furiously. His eyes darted as they fired rapid commands to his SmartGlasses.

'Guys,' JJ said, 'this is too freaky—we need to tell someone. We—'

'Listen,' Zander said, cutting in. 'I searched "Khufu" and "Suez". Listen to this: "The fourth dynasty King established Egypt's first commercial harbour on the Gulf of Suez four and a half thousand years ago."'

Mila frowned. 'It fits—Khufu, bolt, two attacks.'

'Yup,' JJ gulped. 'All the more reason to alert the authorities!'

'But who?' Isabel asked.

JJ shook his head. 'The CIA, Mossad, MI5—somebody!'

Isabel pulled at her hair. 'But how do we know who to trust if we don't know who's involved?'

Zander was nodding. 'Who's to say they would even believe us? They might think *we* sent the symbols.'

'We can show them we got them *before* the attacks on Egypt,' JJ said.

'Time stamps can be faked,' Zander said with a shrug. 'Also...'

'Also?' JJ prompted.

'Also, we cannot forget,' Zander continued, 'that just a few hours ago we thought *Felix* sent us the First Sign.'

Mila's green eyes glittered. 'You are not saying he does this?'

'I am not saying that,' Zander replied. 'But the authorities might think that—after all, you said yourself that he is the common link between us all.'

Mila bit her lip.

'If anyone thought he was involved . . . we'd lose everything, our prizes, our SpaceSkimmer trips,' JJ said.

Zander nodded. 'I think we should try to work out the remaining symbols and speak to Andy and Dylan, and especially Yasmin, before we decide who to tell. We have to be sure . . . really, really sure. I will keep trying Yasmin and call back as soon as I know anything more, all right?'

After the girls had said anxious farewells to JJ and Zander, Pablo arrived with their breakfast.

'What is this?' Mila asked, glad to have something else to talk about for a moment.

'*Calentado*—beans, rice, sausage and bread,' Isabel said, looking at the big plate in front of her. 'Your bowl is *changua*—egg soup. Why don't we share?'

The girls ate half-heartedly as the wall screens showed updates from Egypt. The most worrying footage was of Giza in turmoil as police and looters clashed.

'Maybe Yasmin was already at the airport, yes?' Mila speculated hopefully, setting aside the plate as her appetite deserted her completely.

'I can't stand this,' Isabel said, tying her pink hair back in a ponytail. 'I'm calling Miss Chen.'

Mila stiffened a little. 'But we agreed—'

'Don't worry,' Isabel said tersely. 'I'm not going to say anything about the symbols. But surely Felix Scott's right-hand woman can find out what's going on with Yasmin!'

Mila nodded.

A moment later, Isabel had Miss Chen on her phone, looking as cool and calm as ever behind her SmartGlasses.

'Girls,' she said, lips pursed. 'Is everything all right in Bogotá?'

'Better than it is in Cairo,' Isabel replied.

'You have spoken to Yasmin?' Mila asked hopefully.

'Not yet,' Miss Chen said. 'The Egyptian phone system is down. But rest assured we are keeping tabs on the situation.'

'What is this "keeping tabs"?' Mila asked.

Miss Chen paused as if thinking of how to explain the phrase. 'It means we are keeping an eye on developments.'

A chill went through Mila.

'Can we speak to Felix?' Isabel asked.

'He cannot be disturbed right now,' Miss Chen replied. 'But I have dispatched some of our security people in Cairo to make sure Yasmin is OK.'

Isabel sighed with relief. 'You've got people there?'

Miss Chen offered her thin version of a smile. 'Infinity Corporation has three million employees. We have people *everywhere*.' Her eyes flicked as she checked other displays on her SmartGlasses. 'Girls, I have to go. I will be in contact when I know more about Yasmin.'

With that, Felix's assistant disconnected the call. The girls looked at each other over their half-eaten breakfasts.

'Doesn't sound like she knows much more than we do,' Isabel said. 'But it's good they're trying to ensure Yasmin's safety.'

'"Keeping an eye on developments"?' Mila said. '*Eye*—like the symbol—a little freaky, yes?'

Isabel let out a nervous laugh. 'Now you're being paranoid.'

'I hope so,' Mila said.

A group of Isabel's art friends swept into the cafe and joined the girls at their table. After being introduced, Mila found herself on the edge of a heated debate about what had happened in Egypt.

'"Offline",' argued one boy. 'That's what the pilot said—it sounds like an accident.'

'But the missile *wasn't* offline, was it?' countered a girl. 'It looked like it was right on target!'

The boy shrugged and sipped his coffee. 'Maybe that was just . . . bad luck?'

'What?' the girl scoffed. 'Just like that big ship catching fire right at the same time. Puh-lease!'

'Maybe the plane and boat had the same software systems?' the boy came back.

'Rubbish!' the girl replied. 'The question is, who did this and why? What do you think, Isabel?'

Mila tensed as she glanced at her friend. She could see

Isabel struggling to keep their secret. What would these Colombian kids think if they showed them the symbols? Would they say Isabel and Mila were crazy to think they meant anything? Or would they see them as evidence of an evil conspiracy?

'I think,' Isabel said, setting her phone face-down on the table as if to resist the temptation to show what it held, 'that we should wait to find out more before jumping to conclusions.'

That triggered a new debate—about how much the media would ever tell people about what was *really* going on.

'You're quiet,' said an older boy with a shaved head and an arm sleeve of bright tattoos, as he sat by Mila. 'Don't have an opinion?'

She felt her cheeks go pink.

'What are you drawing there?' he asked, leaning closer.

Mila hadn't even been aware that she was doodling on the paper tablecloth. Now she realised she had drawn her symbol.

'Is that your tag?' he queried.

'Tag?'

When the guy chuckled, Mila saw he had a gold front tooth. Shaved head, arm tattoos, bling dentistry: talk about trying hard for an arty image!

'A tag is your graffiti signature,' he said pleasantly, looking around the cafe. 'Half these kids are graffiti artists.

My tag is Bender.' He grabbed a crayon and did an admittedly clever cartoon version of himself and scrawled 'BNDR' underneath.

'Very good,' Mila said. This guy seemed nice despite his too-cool-for-school vibe.

'*Gracias.*' His eyes went back to her symbol. 'So what is that?'

'I, er, don't know,' Mila said. 'Sorry.'

'You know what it looks like to me?'

Mila peered at him.

'A paragraph mark,' he said. 'You know, like when you turn on the formatting symbols on a computer document.'

Mila looked from Bender to the tablecloth—and saw exactly what he meant!

'Thank you!' she blurted, forgetting her shyness.

Bender gave her a puzzled smile.

'Excuse me, please,' Mila said, glancing at her phone. 'I need to check something.'

The guy gestured for her to go ahead and watched curiously as she whipped out her phone.

Mila angled herself away from Bender and did an internet search on 'paragraph mark symbol'. A moment later, her screen held dozens of variations on the image. There were sleek new ones from modern computer programs and elaborate older versions from medieval manuscripts.

Heart thumping, mouth dry, Mila grabbed Isabel's arm.

'Ow, what?' her friend snapped.

'Come with me,' Mila said, glancing back at Bender, who

gave her a glinting gold smile.

They found an empty table in the corner.

'Look,' Mila said, handing over her phone. 'My symbol is a paragraph mark.'

Isabel's eyes danced with excitement. 'You're right,' she said. 'I can't believe it. They're all over electronic documents but you never pay them any attention. Quick, what does it mean?'

The girls huddled over the phone as Mila did another search and found an entry on a blog called WerdNerdz.

Pilcrow

The paragraph mark is properly known as a 'pilcrow' and dates back to the 1400s. It was originally used in medieval manuscripts to tell the reader that a new idea was being introduced into the text. Such changes in subject were later indicated by the paragraph break. These days pilcrows mainly exist as ghosts in word-processing programs. They remain hidden unless you click the show button, then they'll appear whenever your press the return key.

The pilcrow is also known as an alinea, which is Latin for 'off the line'.

'"Off the line",' Mila said. 'Doesn't that sound like what the Egyptian pilot said? "Offline"?'

Isabel gulped and nodded. She hunched over the paper on the table and quickly sketched the symbols, scribbling words underneath each.

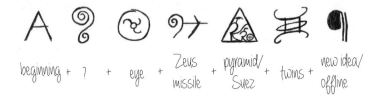

'OK,' Isabel said. 'I'm officially scared now.'

Mila sat on her hands to keep them from shaking. 'So what does the spiral mean?' she whispered.

Yasmin wondered if she should tell her parents about the symbols and website that seemed to have something to do with the attacks. But how on earth could she possibly explain it without sounding like she was making it up—or crazy?

'A sunken ship this size is difficult to move,' a reporter was saying now as the *Futura* burned low in the Suez Canal behind her. 'It might be weeks or months before this vital waterway is open again. Speculation is already mounting that this disaster is linked to the shocking event at the Great Pyramid.'

'Of course they are linked!' Mr Adib said angrily. 'Any fool can see that!'

The TV went off and the lights went out. Everyone gasped as the lounge room fell into darkness. They were used to blackouts in Cairo but the timing of this one only added to the feeling that the world was going insane. To make matters worse, Yasmin's phone showed that Egypt's network was down. She chided herself for not calling the DARE winners back when she had the chance. They might have been able to tell her something more. Surely they had also realised the symbols of the First Sign were connected to what had just happened.

'I'll get my little TV,' Radha was saying.

The family sat, looking at each other fearfully, listening

to the horns, sirens and shouting from out in the street.

Radha returned with her wind-up television. She gave it a few cranks and picked up a fuzzy black-and-white picture.

'. . . while the pyramid attack will be devastating for tourism,' a financial expert was saying gloomily, 'the Suez Canal incident will have much worse consequences. It's the waterway that oil tankers and cargo ships use to go from Europe to Asia without having to go around Africa. If it's closed for a long time, Egypt's economy could be ruined. That, in turn, could cause a global economic collapse.'

'Listen!' Radha said, turning the TV volume down.

Someone was rattling the shop's shutter, trying to get in!

Yasmin saw grim determination in her father's eyes as he took Radha's silver pistol from his pocket.

'Call your brothers back again!' he said to his wife.

Mrs Adib stabbed at her phone. 'It's useless—the network is still down! Even if I could get through, they're on the other side of town!'

'The children,' Radha urged, 'we must get them away!'

Mr Adib looked gravely at Mahmoud. 'I will protect your mother and grandmother and the shop,' he said, 'but you must get your sister to the airport. Put her on Felix's plane, and tell them you want to chaperone her. Insist if you must! Go, now! Take the jeep and—'

Mahmoud shook his head and jabbed a finger at the TV. 'I can't, Dad—look!'

The screen's aerial view of Giza and Cairo showed all major roads jammed with taxis, tour buses, police and tanks.

Angry voices erupted outside the shop. Then came shots and screams.

'Mahmoud, your bike!' Mrs Adib said. 'Go by the back streets. You might get through. Go!'

'Do as your mother says,' Mr Adib commanded. 'I will hold them in the shop.'

Yasmin's eyes burned with tears. She didn't want to leave her family like this but she knew she was powerless to help.

Mr Adib gave her and Mahmoud quick hugs. 'Son, daughter—go! Call us when you can.'

With that, he strode, chest out, from the lounge room and into the shop. 'Get away from here!' he shouted. 'I'm armed.'

'Come on!' Mrs Adib whispered. 'You have to go!'

Yasmin slung her backpack over her shoulder and followed her mother out to the small backyard.

Mahmoud eased his powerful bike to the rear gate.

'Be careful!' Mrs Adib sobbed, throwing her arms around her son and daughter, while Radha looked on snuffling.

'Don't worry, Mother,' Mahmoud said. 'I've got this. Here, sister.'

Yasmin shook her head as he offered her his new helmet and leather jacket.

'I insist,' he said.

'No time to argue, girl!' Radha said. 'Put them on!'

Yasmin pulled them on and climbed onto the motorbike behind Mahmoud. Hot tears pricked her eyes but she forced herself to be brave as her mother opened the gate that led to the back alley.

'OK, sis,' Mahmoud said, twisting the throttle so the engine revved powerfully. 'Ready?'

Yasmin imagined the map in her head. From here, they had to go back around the corner, navigate dozens of Giza's tight alleys, cross one of the many bridges over the Nile River, get through central Cairo and then go out past Heliopolis to the airport. It felt like mission impossible.

'Here we go,' Mahmoud said.

With a final nod to their mother and grandmother, he shot the bike out into the bumpy lane and weaved between panicking locals using it as an escape route. Yasmin was shocked at what she saw when her brother skidded to a stop at the corner a few doors down from their shop. Their entire street was in chaos. It was so much worse at ground level than it had looked on TV. Stores that weren't shuttered had smashed windows. Groups of masked men ran with whatever they could carry. Cars and buses were rammed up close to each other, horns honking, drivers yelling, terrified passengers whimpering behind windows.

Yasmin had no idea how they would ever get through this dangerous mess alive.

A police chopper swooped overhead, speakers blaring, ordering residents to return to their homes.

'Brother,' she shouted, 'maybe we should do what they say—go back to our house and—'

The words died in Yasmin's throat. Through the bitter smoke curling down the street, she spotted ... *Jackal*!

The detective and his minions were outside their store.

There were two crumpled bodies at their feet. That's what the shots and screams had been just a minute ago. Jackal and his gang had murdered those people! Now he was yelling at his thugs to use a fallen telegraph pole as a battering ram on the shutter.

'Little pig, let me come in!' he shouted at the door.

Yasmin couldn't believe it! In all this madness, Jackal still wanted to kidnap her. He had no idea she wasn't inside.

'Mahmoud!' she said desperately.

Her brother let out a cry as Jackal's gang—

Crrrruncccch!

—smashed the telegraph pole into the store's shutter.

The blow buckled the metal, leaving an almighty dent. A few more hits like that and Jackal and his gang would be through. Who knew what they would do to her family?

'Mahmoud,' she said. 'We have to draw them away!'

Her brother nodded.

'Jackal, you son of a shoe. Over here!' Yasmin yelled.

The detective whirled around. 'There!' he shouted to his men. 'Quick—get them!'

Jackal lurched for his motorbike as his gang dropped their battering ram and made for their own rides.

Mahmoud twisted the throttle. His bike roared.

'Sister,' he shouted, 'you need to hang on tight now!'

The Signmaker let out a furious cry that echoed through the golden-lit secret headquarters. This wasn't the way things were supposed to happen!

The Egyptian detective had been promised $100,000 to make sure Yasmin stayed safe no matter what else happened today. Half of the money had already been transferred into his account. But the cop would only get the rest when he delivered the DARE Award winner to Cairo's airport safely.

Except the satellite image had just shown the detective and his men trying to smash their way into the Adib family's store. Now they were chasing Yasmin and her brother on motorbikes. A quick hack into the Adib security-camera system provided an audio recording of the kidnapping attempt. The detective had gotten greedy. Clearly he hoped to make a lot more money by holding Yasmin for ransom.

The Signmaker vowed that the detective wouldn't see another cent. Instead he would pay for his betrayal.

It would be a simple matter to expose the man's corruption with a single email to his more honest police colleagues. But they wouldn't catch him before he caught Yasmin. And that wouldn't be nearly punishment enough for jeopardising the Signmaker's carefully laid plans.

The Signmaker checked satellite positions but the nearest hackable space laser was orbiting over Iran, nowhere near enough to blow Jackal and his men off their bikes. Throwing one of the police helicopters in the skies over Cairo at them was a possibility, but there was no guarantee of hitting any of the speeding targets.

The Signmaker took a deep breath, setting aside feelings of fury and frustration. Obstacles were opportunities. Challenges produced strength. Strength was power. There *had* to be a way to stop the detective and his cops.

While their motorbikes were too primitive to be hacked, any AutoDrive cars around them *could* be controlled remotely. Cairo didn't have that many driverless vehicles yet, but there had to be a few in the area that could be used.

Face set with a smile, fingers flying across a keyboard, screens flashing new feeds and information, the Signmaker was determined to regain control—at any cost.

Mahmoud gunned the bike between cars, blasting the horn to scatter people from their path. He steered around a camel with a screaming tourist stuck in its saddle, and shot the motorbike into an alley.

Clinging to her brother, Yasmin looked over her shoulder to see the cops trying to follow, angling between vehicles to the fury of drivers. One cop had already been cut off, his machine screeching, caught hopelessly between the fender of a BMW and the bumper bar of a tour bus. But Jackal was through the dense traffic, silver sunglasses glinting, mad grimace on his face, with the remaining three of his gang close behind him.

'Go! Go! Go!' Yasmin urged, holding on tighter as Mahmoud accelerated.

Walls flashed by. Eyes peered from dark doorways. Houses exhaled cooking aromas. Mahmoud zipped around a donkey cart, the driver smiling toothlessly at Yasmin. Their bike roared by a cafe's empty outside tables and they just avoided smacking into a burning mini-van as they sped around a blind corner. But when Yasmin looked back, she saw Jackal and his convoy of thugs mimicking Mahmoud's every move.

Yasmin didn't know what they'd do if Jackal and his men turned on their sirens. To anyone on the streets, it would look like she and her brother were bad guys fleeing from the cops! But the lack of sirens made Yasmin wonder if Jackal didn't want to draw too much attention. Otherwise he'd be calling those helicopters hovering over Giza to join in the chase.

At least he can't risk shooting me, she thought. *I'm no good to him dead. I hope.*

Glancing back, Yasmin was glad to see one of Jackal's men stuck in the middle of a small herd of goats that had stampeded from a laneway.

'Lean with me!' shouted Mahmoud. Yasmin did and he angled them low around another corner. When he righted the machine, they were zooming along a garbage-strewn street beneath ugly concrete apartment buildings.

Mahmoud didn't slow or stop as they approached a major boulevard, even though its two southbound lanes were bumper-to-bumper with cars. Instead, he sped up.

'Hang on!' he called over his shoulder.

Yasmin clung to him for her life as Mahmoud pulled the bike up onto its back wheel and jumped it onto a car bonnet. Even as it crunched beneath their weight, her brother popped another wheelie and launched them onto the hood of the next car. Its driver screaming, he hopped the bike down onto the green nature strip.

Amid horns and shouts, he revved wildly, scattering pigeons and onlookers. A second later they shot across the northbound lanes, just missing a motorcycle taxi, before disappearing into the shadows of a side street.

Barely able to breathe, let alone believe she was still alive, Yasmin cast a glance backwards. Jackal was still in the traffic, angrily shouting at drivers to move, his men not going anywhere on their bikes.

Yasmin allowed herself a quick grin, hoping they'd lose Jackal and his thugs once and for all as they sped towards the Nile.

But what she saw next shocked her. The detective and his men had left their bikes and were running up and over cars. Just before she and Mahmoud rounded a corner, Yasmin glimpsed her pursuers holding up their guns and badges, ordering a group of men stopped at the traffic lights to give up their motorbikes.

Yasmin gasped as the horrible truth dawned on her—Jackal wasn't going to give up easily . . . or maybe ever.

Bang-bang-bang!

Andy's heart thumped in his chest. This couldn't be happening. Beard Dude and Bald Guy—they were in his bedroom doorway, guns raised, shooting at him!

Bang-bang-bang!

Andy jolted awake, panting, pulse racing. With a start he realised the banging was just someone knocking on his bedroom door. The real noise had become part of his unreal nightmare.

'It's Daniels,' a voice said. 'Wake up.'

Officer Jake Daniels worked with Andy's dad. The young policeman swung open the bedroom door and turned on the light.

Sitting up in bed, sandy hair all over the place, Andy blinked in the glare.

'What's happening?' Dylan murmured from the floor, reaching for his glasses. 'What time is it?'

'Nearly seven,' said Daniels. 'Andy, your dad's been trying to call you. You need to get on the phone to him. He said it's urgent.'

Andy nodded. If his dad had been at LAPD headquarters all night and was calling urgently, he hoped it could only mean that Beard Dude and Bald Guy had been caught and were behind bars.

'I'll call him,' Andy said. 'OK if I go to the toilet first?'

Daniels nodded. 'Sure, but make it quick.'

As Andy went down the hall, Dylan sat up, stretched and yawned. Blinking and bleary-eyed, he unrolled his phone and scrolled to the Games Thinker website.

11:01:54

The timer had reset while they'd slept.

'Wonder what happened to the First Sign,' Dylan muttered sleepily. 'Events for you as blah, blah, blah.'

'Guess you guys won't know?' Daniels interrupted Dylan's musings.

'Know what now?' Dylan asked, looking up at the frowning policeman.

'About Egypt,' the policeman said glumly. 'Someone blew up a big pyramid and a huge boat sank in the Suez Canal.'

'What?' Dylan said.

Daniels nodded. His patrol radio crackled and he stepped into the hall to answer it.

Dylan's eyes flew to his phone. He had missed several calls overnight. There were also texts from JJ and Isabel. He scrolled to JJ's, fearing it would be terrible news about Yasmin. But it wasn't. Even with Egypt in chaos, JJ was still worried about decoding the First Sign? But Dylan's blood ran cold as what he read sank in.

correct order of symbols

numbers = coordinates for Great Pyramid of Giza

29.9792° N, 31.1344° E

countdown = zero = missile attack

Barely able to believe what he had just seen, Dylan scrolled to Isabel's message.

> Mila's symbol is a pilcrow.
>
> Means 'a new thought' or 'offline'.
>
> 'Offline' is what the Egyptian pilot screamed!
>
> Call when you wake up.

'What's going on?' Andy asked when he returned to the bedroom and saw Dylan's shocked expression.

'Quick,' the Aussie barked. 'Turn on the news!'

'Holo on,' said Andy. The bedroom's HoloSpace came to life. 'News.'

Horrified and fascinated, the boys watched as jet fighters circled the pyramids and soldiers with guns surrounded the Sphinx. A news ticker brought them up to speed in short, sharp sentences:

PYRAMID ATTACKED BY MISSILE,

13 DEAD, 100s INJURED;

SHIP DESTROYED IN SUEZ CANAL;

EGYPTIAN GOVT DECLARES STATE OF EMERGENCY.

'Man, this is *bad*,' Andy said. 'I hope Yasmin's all right.'

'Me, too, but it gets worse,' Dylan said with an audible gulp. 'While we were asleep, the other guys figured out that if you put all the symbols and numbers of the First Sign together, it's a ...'

'A what?'

'A *prediction*. "The First Sign" *predicted* what was going to happen in Egypt!'

Andy's jaw fell open.

'The timer counted it down exactly!' Dylan added.

Andy shook his head. 'You're kidding, right?'

'Check your messages,' Dylan urged. 'See for yourself.'

Grabbing his phone, Andy sat on the edge of his bed. After reading for a few moments, he looked up with wide eyes. 'This is crazy.'

'We've got to call the others,' Dylan said. 'And we've *got* to find out where Yasmin is in all of ... that chaos.'

'Andy!' said Daniels, reappearing in the doorway. 'You gotta call your dad. That was him on the radio. He sounds ...'

'Sounds?'

'Angry.'

'Huh? Sure, OK, Daniels.'

Andy was starting to get a bad feeling about the day. His normally sunny face clouded over as a heavy dread settled in his stomach.

The traffic became thicker as Mahmoud and Yasmin got closer to the Nile. It was as if everyone in Giza had decided it'd be safer to cross into central Cairo. Not that doing so really made any sense. The attack had been from a jet, just like the dozens of jets screaming in circles over the city now, and that meant nowhere was safe.

Mahmoud put down the kickstand, stood up on his bike seat and looked east over the car roofs. The traffic on Abbas Bridge was a solid wall.

'Up that way,' he said, pointing further up the Nile. 'We have to be able to get across one of the other bridges.'

Yasmin looked around desperately at the cars crowding them in all directions. The noise was deafening, the fumes choking, but at least she couldn't see Jackal's mirrored sunglasses anywhere.

'No sign of him,' she said hopefully. 'I hope his fleas turn into cobras and bite him all over.'

Mahmoud laughed. It was another one of their grandmother's colourful insults.

When a car beside them crawled forward enough to create a gap, Mahmoud seized the opportunity to turn the motorbike onto a side street. They drove past Cairo University, where Yasmin hoped to study when she finished school in a few years, and Giza Zoo, whose monkey house was the first thing she ever remembered in her life.

'This isn't much better,' Mahmoud said, angling the bike up a pedestrian ramp, honking the horn and edging between people who seemed to be carrying everything they owned. 'Impossible! Everyone should stay inside.'

'What?' Yasmin asked with a grin. 'Like us?'

To their right, the Nile River glittered between the palm trees along its bank, and up ahead Cairo Tower rose above the greenery of Gezira Island. A few military and police boats thudded this way and that across the waters, blaring orders for *felucca* sailing boats and cargo barges to pull into shore for their own safety.

Mahmoud threaded the motorbike through cars until they were almost on the Cairo University Bridge. But the eastbound lanes heading into the city were packed solid with honking cars and trucks. No-one was moving. Only the westbound lanes were flowing with vehicles whose drivers were foolish enough to be heading towards Giza.

'At least that dirty cop doesn't know where we're going,' Mahmoud said.

Yasmin's heart skipped a beat.

In the weeks since the DARE Awards, it had been widely reported that she would be travelling on Felix Scott's SpaceSkimmer this week.

'But, brother,' she said. 'Jackal *might* know we're going to the airport because of the media.'

When Mahmoud turned to reply, his eyes went wide with surprise.

'Oh, no!' he gasped.

Yasmin didn't have to look around to know what he'd seen. She held on as Mahmoud made the only move he could. With a twist of the motorbike throttle, he speared the machine up onto the bridge's crash barrier. A second later, like a tightrope act, they were roaring along the thin wall of concrete that separated traffic lanes. There was just enough space for the width of the tyres, so any false move would be their last.

Yasmin quickly glanced back.

Jackal and his thugs were weaving through the traffic, and coming straight for them.

'Dad, it's me,' Andy said, Dylan at his shoulder.

On the phone's screen, Frank Freeman frowned. 'About time,' he said.

'Dad, you know what's happening in Egypt, right?'

His father nodded. 'I know, it's terrible, and I'm sure you're worried about your friend Yasmin, but—'

'No, Dad, we—'

'No! You need to listen to *me* now, OK?'

Andy was shocked by his dad's abrupt tone. He had rarely seen his father so angry.

'This concerns you, too, Dylan,' Frank said. 'So listen up.'

The boys were all ears.

'At the crack of dawn this morning, the guys in your video came into the station. They'd found out about the story on your website and—'

'And they gave themselves up!' Andy said. 'That's great. I knew—'

'Quiet!' Frank said. 'Son, listen to me. I'm trying to protect you. Both of you.'

Andy gulped. *Protect* them? From what? If Beard Dude and Bald Guy were in custody then they were safe. *Unless* their gangster bosses had called in hit men. They could probably do that as easily as sending out for pizza. Assassins might be coming to kill him and Dylan right now!

'Take *Scoop* offline,' Frank demanded. 'Immediately!'

'What? Dad, are we safe?'

'Just do what I say!'

'But if—' Andy said.

His dad shook his head. 'No ifs, no buts. Just do it.'

'Dad, I can't—'

'Andy!' Frank's eyes burned through the phone. 'I am your father. I love you. Trust me. You need to do this right now. For all of us.'

Dylan put his hand on Andy's shoulder. 'Mate,' he said, 'I think you'd better do what he says.'

Andy nodded. 'All right.'

Frank's expression eased a little. 'Good,' he said. 'How long will it take?'

Andy shrugged. 'A few minutes.'

He couldn't believe this. Thanks to Felix's tweet, the *Scoop* story was already a runaway success. But taking it offline now meant millions of people would get a 'Website Not Found' message when they tried to see what all the fuss was about. What a waste—not to mention embarrassing.

'OK,' his father said. 'As soon as that's done, you guys come to the station with Daniels.'

With that gruff order, Andy's dad disconnected the call.

'What's going on?' Dylan asked, face screwed up with worry.

'I have *no* idea. But the old man's as serious as a heart attack.'

Sitting at his computer, Andy started typing the

passwords and commands he needed to deactivate *Scoop*.

'This sucks,' he muttered. 'If the First Sign really did predict what happened in Egypt, then *Scoop*'s the place for the story. It'd be the exclusive of the century!'

Dylan nodded. 'Mate, yeah, but—'

'But?'

'Think about who we thought sent the symbols to us?'

Tapping away, Andy nodded grimly. 'Yeah, you're right. If our first thought was Felix, then everyone else's will be too. But there's no way he's got anything to do with this! I mean, why would he?'

'I know,' said Dylan, 'but people even *thinking* there's a link could ruin him and Infinity Corporation, as well as the DARE Awards.'

'You're right,' Andy sighed, hitting the return key. 'OK, *Scoop*'s offline.'

He looked at the Egyptian footage on the HoloSpace. The news now showed the smoking ruin of the *Futura* in the Suez Canal. The feeling everyone was in for a very bad day swept over him again.

Yasmin clung to Mahmoud as he raced the motorbike along the top of the bridge's concrete divider. Traffic was banked up on their right but cars and trucks whizzed by in the lanes to their left. While Yasmin had faith in her brother's riding skills, she knew that one slip here would be deadly. But slowing down wasn't an option. The crooked cops had copied Mahmoud's daredevil move. They were following along the narrow crash barrier, Jackal bringing up the rear.

Mahmoud blasted his horn.

Up ahead, their path was blocked. Drivers stuck in traffic had gotten out of their cars and were sitting on the divider while they played cards.

Mahmoud slowed down. 'Move!'

The men glanced up from their game and shrugged. Behind them, Jackal and his men were gaining.

'Time to play chicken!' Mahmoud yelled back to Yasmin. 'Hang on!'

'No!' she heard herself cry. 'Don't!'

Her brother didn't listen. Instead, he angled the bike, twisted the throttle and jumped the machine off the crash barrier into the busy lanes of oncoming traffic. The driver of a van yelled behind his windshield as their motorbike raced at him. But Mahmoud kept his cool, swerving skilfully, shooting them between the van and a speeding lorry in the next lane, with just inches to spare on either side. A split second later the deadly game of dodge began all over again. Looming ahead was a blue car. Its driver honked his horn furiously. But Mahmoud steered them out of harm's way safely. He weaved in and out of the approaching traffic again and again before a bus forced him back close to the crash barrier. A furious torrent of vehicles followed, keeping them near the concrete divider.

Yasmin's heart sank. The cops must have cleared the card players as they were now racing along the barrier, gaining speed because they didn't have to dodge vehicles.

A cop was almost alongside Mahmoud's bike. Jackal was right behind. But the other cop had jumped his bike off the divider and was chasing them on the road.

'Faster!' Yasmin urged Mahmoud.

But his bike was going at full speed.

Pow-zing!

Sparks flew off the ground just ahead. Yasmin whirled. The cop on the road was riding one-handed and aiming his pistol at their tyres. He might not miss next time. She knew a blow-out at this speed would—

An AutoDrive car abruptly veered out of its lane just after it passed them. Yasmin glimpsed the passengers' surprised faces in the windows as they realised their vehicle was out of control. An instant later the sedan—

Ba-crump!

—smacked into the cop's motorbike head on.

The man didn't have a chance. He and his motorbike

were flung high into the air in a cloud of shrieking metal and shattered glass.

Yasmin didn't have time to feel sorry for him. Through her shock she saw the other cop was closing in along the crash barrier. Steering his bike with one hand, he had his gun in the other.

Ba-bang!

The bullet whizzed by Yasmin and ricocheted off the road with a loud ping. The cop grinned. He took aim again. Yasmin had to fight back. But with what? Then she remembered. *Radha's present!* Reaching into her pocket, she pulled out the vial of sand. Yanking out the cork stopper with her teeth, she shook it like a wand at the cop.

The man screamed as the sudden sandstorm swept into his eyes. Blinded, he spun out of control, he and his motorbike tumbled off the barrier and crunched into the stationary cars in the eastbound lanes.

Then, as if by magic, the road ahead cleared. Mahmoud swerved smoothly across empty lanes and onto a ramp that led down into another of Cairo's riverside avenues. Yasmin saw Jackal stop on the crash barrier behind them. He was waving his badge and gun to halt traffic so he could continue the chase. Even with his men scattered, injured and likely dead, the corrupt detective wasn't calling it quits.

Brrrrt!

Yasmin's phone vibrated in her pocket. The network was back up. Road rushing by, holding Mahmoud with one arm, she pulled out her phone and saw the caller was Miss Chen.

'Accept,' she yelled.

Miss Chen's calm face appeared on the screen in her SmartGlasses. 'Yasmin,' she said. 'Are you all right?'

'Not all right,' Yasmin gasped.

'Where are you?'

'Back of my brother's motorbike.'

Miss Chen frowned behind her SmartGlasses. 'I sent some men to assist. Did they make contact?'

For a terrible moment, Yasmin thought Miss Chen was talking about Jackal. Then she realised. The two men that were killed outside her family store had worked for Felix!

'If they're who I think,' Yasmin said, leaning with the bike as Mahmoud zipped between cars, 'they . . . didn't make it.'

'Are you saying they are dead?'

Yasmin nodded.

Miss Chen didn't miss a beat. 'I am tracking your phone on our computer system. Are you heading to the airport?'

'Yes,' Yasmin said. She glanced over her shoulder once more. A few blocks back, Jackal was racing off the bridge and down the ramp. The man was unstoppable.

'Negative,' Miss Chen said, eyes registering new info on her SmartGlasses. 'Cairo Airport has just been closed. All flights are being diverted.'

'Diverted?' Yasmin said. 'Where?'

'Alexandria,' Miss Chen said. 'I can reroute your SpaceSkimmer and meet you there myself.'

Yasmin had been to Egypt's second-biggest city for a beach holiday when she was ten. It was a three-hour drive from Cairo. There was no way they could ride all that way north. Not with Jackal on their tail.

'Or you can wait until Cairo Airport's open again?' Miss Chen offered.

'We can't,' Yasmin said. 'The guy who killed your men is after us. He wants to kidnap me.'

'We'll get Yasmin to Alexandria!' Mahmoud shouted. 'Just be there!'

Miss Chen nodded. 'I will make su—'

Yasmin's phone screen went blank and then the words 'No Service' flashed up.

She tucked her phone back in her pocket and clung tighter to her brother.

'We have to lose Jackal if we're going to get to Alexandria,' he said loudly.

'The Old City!' Yasmin yelled.

Her brother nodded and swung the motorbike off the main boulevard and onto a smaller road. From there, the streets cut haphazardly between tightly packed shops and markets, mosques and houses. Losing themselves in this maze might be their best chance of evading Jackal.

With a series of sharp turns, Mahmoud took them along lanes that became narrower and more lost in the shadows beneath ancient buildings. But no matter how many twists and turns they made, whenever Yasmin looked around she saw Jackal, just a block behind or storming around a corner, always following relentlessly.

'I can't shake him,' Mahmoud said, seeing the cop in his

side-view mirror, 'but I've got another idea.'

Her brother twisted the throttle and pushed the bike to its limit. The burst of power put a bit more distance between them and Jackal, who'd been slowed down by a donkey cart and was shouting at the owner to get out of the way.

Racing around a corner, Mahmoud skidded to a stop. He jumped out of his seat and held the bike so Yasmin could hop off.

'Quick!' he said. 'Give me the helmet, the jacket and the backpack!'

Yasmin understood. She shook her head. 'No, Mahmoud, we have to stick together.'

'There's no time,' he said. 'I can outrun him. Come on!'

Yasmin did as he asked. Her brother let his precious bike fall with a clang so it looked like they'd crashed. He pulled on the red jacket, yellow helmet and threw the backpack over his shoulder.

'Hide behind that,' Mahmoud said, pointing at an old rusted car. 'When it's clear, get to the railway station. You can make it to Alexandria in a few hours by train.'

Yasmin squeezed his shoulder. 'Be safe, brother!'

Mahmoud grinned. He almost looked like he was enjoying himself.

'Take care, sister,' he said. 'Send me a postcard!'

With that, he ran off. Yasmin ducked behind the rusty car just before Jackal rounded the corner.

'I see you, girl!' he shouted.

For a moment, Yasmin thought their trick hadn't worked,

but then Jackal revved his bike and roared away. Daring to peek from her hiding spot, she saw her brother clambering across a rooftop, the bright colours of his jacket and helmet popping against the late-afternoon sky. From a distance, Mahmoud looked like her. Jackal certainly thought so, because the corrupt cop was off his bike and scaling a wall in pursuit.

A minute later, they were both out of sight. Yasmin prayed her brother would get away and that his clumsiness wouldn't betray him. She stayed crouched in her hiding spot, paralysed by fear, until she noticed that the sky above was beginning to blaze with sunset colours. Yasmin had to move. She had to get to the railway station! She forced herself to stand up and brushed the dust from her clothes. But which way was it?

Yasmin looked around and noticed the strange doorway next to her. Her heart skittered. If she didn't know better, she'd swear she was standing outside . . . a tomb!

That's because it *was* a tomb.

In fact, there were tombs everywhere. Then the realisation hit her.

Yasmin might have escaped Jackal. But now she was lost, deep in the legendary City of the Dead.

It was getting dark.

Trying to control her panic, Yasmin starting walking through the eerie City of the Dead. While there were tombs everywhere, some ancient, others modern, almost all of them bore signs of . . . life.

Yasmin had heard about this place. For centuries, Cairo's poorest people had made their homes inside and around these tombs. All Egyptians knew about it but few ever ventured there, scared off by spooky stories of murderers and ghosts.

She didn't see either. Instead, from inside an open crypt, she saw the flicker of a television, while lilting music drifted from another. She smelled cooking fires and heard children laughing. Washing hung from lines above gravestones. Power cords looped across the tomb roofs. Despite the sprawling cemetery's foreboding name, this was very much a city of the living.

'Hello, miss, pen?'

Yasmin spun around, startled, and saw a skinny boy holding out his hand. Her heart melted even though she was no stranger to beggars—Cairo had more than its fair share. She wished she had a pen to give this little boy. But all she had were the clothes on her back and her phone and passport.

'Sorry, I have no pen today,' she said. 'But can you tell me which way to the railway station?'

The boy blinked. Yasmin wondered whether he understood. She didn't know whether children raised in the City of the Dead even went to school. And she felt sure they didn't take trains very often.

'You know, trains?' she said. 'You know, choo-choo?'

The boy nodded eagerly. 'You come. This way, OK?'

Yasmin followed him as he skipped through a nearby archway that led into a courtyard. They walked across and down a lane that wound between crypts, chickens scattering ahead of them. A scrawny dog ran alongside for a while, before realising she had no food to offer. Then the boy led her into another alley lined with shadowy doorways, rough walls and wooden shutters. After a while, everything looked the same. Yasmin's sense of direction was all mixed up and she feared this boy was taking her ever deeper into this maze.

She steeled herself against the fear that he was being used as a lure by people who meant her harm.

'Is this the right way?' she asked nervously.

The boy stopped. He nodded and smiled as he pointed at the entrance of a tomb. It was just like dozens of others they had passed.

'My house,' he said. 'You come.'

Yasmin tried to control her frustration.

'Choo-choo?' the boy said and made an eating motion. 'You are hungry? Chew-chew?'

Yasmin wanted to scream.

'You look lost,' said a witch-like woman with a walking stick who'd appeared from the shadows. 'Do you want to come in and have some tea?'

All Yasmin wanted was to get to the railway station.

'Yasmin!'

She stiffened. It was *his* voice. Jackal. Somehow he'd realised he was following Mahmoud. Now he sounded close. Just a few courtyards away. 'Where are you?' he called. 'I am going to find you!'

Suddenly having a cup of tea in a tomb house seemed like a very good idea.

'*Shukran*,' Yasmin said, nodding. 'You are very hospitable.'

Yasmin followed the woman and boy into a small dark room. At its centre was an old stone coffin, being used as a table to hold pots, plates and glass jars of rice and beans. Along two walls were rolls of bedding.

'Please, rest,' the woman said, pointing to cushions and mats around a low table.

Yasmin sat farthest from the door, trying to melt into the shadows. But if Jackal poked his head in, there was no doubt she'd be trapped. They didn't make tombs with rear exits. Grinning, the boy plonked down next to her and buried his nose in a comic book.

'My name is Sybil,' the woman said, pouring cups of tea from a steaming pot.

'I'm Yasmin.'

'I know.'

A shiver danced up Yasmin's spine. 'How do you know?'

'Sometimes I see things that others cannot,' Sybil said, chuckling as she sat with their drinks. 'But in this case I saw the look on your face when that man called your name.'

'He's a—a bad cop, trying to kidnap me,' Yasmin blurted out. 'Please, help me.'

Sybil nodded. 'I will. You are among friends here.'

With Daniels at the wheel, the squad car crawled through Los Angeles. Andy and Dylan sat in the back, feeling like common criminals.

'Did you really have to confiscate our phones?' Andy asked.

They'd been stuck in nightmare peak-hour traffic since they left the house so they hadn't been able to call the others.

'Your dad's orders,' Daniels said. 'Sorry.'

'I really need to make a call.'

Daniels shook his head.

'Please, Jake,' Andy said. 'It's urgent. I'll be sixty seconds, tops.'

'On one condition,' Daniels said.

'Anything,' Andy replied.

'Dylan, can your parents sign a photo for my wife? She's a big fan.'

The Aussie boy nodded. 'Yes, sure. I give you my word, I'll make it happen.'

'This is our secret, OK?' Daniels said, handing Andy's phone back. 'Sixty seconds.'

Andy and Dylan put their heads together and called Isabel. She and Mila appeared on the screen.

'We can't talk long,' Andy said. 'Fill me in quick.'

Isabel explained everything they knew—including that no-one had been able to contact Yasmin.

'We could've stopped the attacks,' Andy whispered angrily, 'if we'd decoded the First Sign in time.'

'I don't think so,' Isabel retorted. 'There's no way we could have figured it out before they happened.'

Mila nodded. 'It only makes sense after, yes?'

Andy shrugged. 'I guess.'

'But what's the timer counting down to now?' Dylan asked.

'We don't know,' Isabel said. 'But answer something for me—why are you in the back of a *police car*?'

Daniels pulled the squad car up in front of the Los Angeles Police Administration Building on First Street. The huge steel and glass structure reflected the city's sunny sky. 'Time to hang up,' he said.

'We're not sure yet,' Andy whispered to Isabel. 'We'll call you back when we can.'

Yasmin sipped her second cup of tea. She was grateful for its warmth and the shelter Sybil had given her from Jackal. But now she needed to keep moving. 'I have to get to the railway station and get a train to Alexandria,' she said.

Sybil whispered to the boy. He jumped up and ran from the house. Yasmin shivered when she thought that maybe the woman had sent him to find Jackal in the hope of a reward.

'Finish your tea so I can see the leaves,' Sybil said.

'You are a fortune teller?' Yasmin asked.

With her white hair and hazel eyes, the woman certainly looked the part.

'Here we do what we can to survive,' Sybil said, taking Yasmin's empty cup. 'My husband looks after tombs for a little money. I read leaves and palms to help buy food.'

Yasmin felt guilty. She'd been raised in luxury and comfort compared with how Sybil and her family lived. And yet she couldn't offer the woman anything. 'I'm sorry, but I have no money to pay you.'

Sybil waved away the apology and stared at the tea leaves. 'You have left your money behind today,' she said. 'But there is great fortune ahead for you.'

Yasmin's eyes widened. Was this woman using magic powers to tell her she'd be getting a million dollars? Or was she just a trickster who'd recognised her from a newspaper article? 'What else do you see?' she asked.

'A desert dog chases you,' Sybil whispered. 'He is not easy to escape.'

Now Yasmin shivered. A jackal was a desert dog!

Her heart thudded as a dark shape appeared in the doorway. For a moment she thought the boy really had brought Jackal. But the shadow belonged to a different beast—one with long ears and a mane. The donkey snorted and brayed.

'Hello, Sybil,' said an old man, poking his head through the door. 'Someone needs a ride?'

The fortune teller nodded. 'This young girl has a train to catch. But she can't be seen by anyone.' Sybil hobbled to the door, Yasmin jumping up to follow her. Outside, the donkey was hitched to a cart filled with watermelons.

'You'll have to hide among those,' the man said. 'It may take a while because the traffic is so bad and my donkey, he is slow.'

Yasmin nodded. She didn't care if it took all night, so long as she left Jackal clueless about where she was.

'*Shukran*,' she said.

She turned to Sybil and took her hand. 'And thank *you*. I will repay your kindness one day.'

The fortune teller nodded. 'I know you will, child.' As she moved her hand down to lean on her walking stick again, Yasmin noticed the decoration on top of it was a carved spiral. 'Sybil, what is that design?'

'This? It is called a *lituus*,' the woman said. 'Ancient priests used it to watch how birds flew through the sky. They predicted the future from what they saw.'

Yasmin pulled out her phone and showed the spiral symbol to Sybil. 'Is it the same as this?'

The old woman peered at the screen. 'Not quite.'

Sybil traced her finger around the spiral on her stick. 'See, mine goes clockwise. That means it foretells what will be created. Yours goes the other way. It predicts what is to be destroyed.'

Fear spiked Yasmin's heart. Destruction! That's what she'd witnessed today. That the symbol was part of the First Sign seemed to confirm her fears it had foretold the terrible events in Egypt.

'Are you all right?' Sybil asked.

Yasmin forced herself to nod.

She climbed up into the donkey cart as the man stacked watermelons over her.

'Fortune be with you, Yasmin,' Sybil whispered.

'Harr!' the man said and the cart pulled away behind the clip-clopping donkey.

They turned one corner, then another, and another. By the time they left the City of the Dead and rumbled onto the clogged Cairo streets, Yasmin had lost track of time.

Above the clamour of honking, a man shouted close behind them.

'Hold it!' Jackal commanded. 'You, donkey man, stop!'

Beneath the fruit, Yasmin's body went rigid with fear.

She heard the crunch of the detective's boots on the dusty street. Through gaps in the watermelons and the cart's wooden planks, Yasmin saw Jackal pass by just centimetres from her.

'You've come from the City of the Dead?' he demanded.

The donkey-cart driver said he had.

'Have you seen this girl?'

Yasmin heard the rustling of newspaper. She guessed Jackal was showing the man her photo in an article about the DARE Awards. She held her breath.

'No,' the man said. 'Rich people don't go there. Only the poor. Would you like to buy a watermelon?'

Jackal didn't say anything for a moment. Yasmin pictured him smelling the air for her scent.

'All right,' he growled. 'Move on, donkey man!'

As the cart lurched forwards, Yasmin silently thanked her lucky stars for the kindness of strangers.

Through the slats, she saw Jackal rubbing his jaw.

'I hope you find the girl,' the driver called out cheerfully.

'I'll find her,' Jackal said, spitting on the ground. 'If it's the last thing I do.'

Andy had visited the seventh-floor LAPD office many times before. As Frank's son, he'd always felt like an honorary cop. But as Daniels led him and Dylan across the squad room, his dad's colleagues either avoided eye contact or gave them solemn looks. Andy didn't understand what he'd done wrong. Then his stomach felt like it was falling away.

'Look,' he hissed to Dylan. 'Corner office.'

Through the glass windows they saw Frank Freeman at a table, talking to Beard Dude and Bald Guy. What could be going on?

Daniels dropped their phones into his desk drawer. 'This way,' he said, leading the boys into a small conference room.

'What do we do now?' Andy queried.

The young officer paused awkwardly by the door. 'Your dad said you're gonna have to just sweat it out. Sorry.' With that, he closed the door.

'Mate, what do you reckon's happening?' Dylan asked.

Andy shook his head as he peered through the blinds. 'Bald Guy and Beard Dude aren't even in handcuffs.'

What he could see in the corner office looked polite. Frank was nodding and listening when he should've been snarling and shouting at those two scumbags.

'I'm not sure what we stumbled into,' Andy said, 'but whatever it is ...'

But Dylan no longer heard him. Instead he was staring with a stunned expression out the conference-room window. Los Angeles smoggy atmosphere had put a halo around the morning sun so that it looked like . . . a fiery dot inside a flaming circle.

Maybe Isabel's symbol *wasn't* an eye!

'Andy,' Dylan said, 'reckon I can ask Daniels a favour?'

Andy shrugged. 'Can't hurt to try. What is it?'

'A hunch,' Dylan said.

Andy opened the door and called out to Daniels, who loped over from his desk.

'Can you look something up on the internet for me?' Dylan asked.

The young cop blinked. 'Uh, I don't know.'

'I'll make sure KitKat write something *really* nice to your wife,' Dylan said smoothly. 'What's her name again?'

'Madison,' Daniels said, hands up. 'OK, OK, what do you need?'

'A dot in a circle,' Dylan said. 'What does that symbol mean?'

Daniels frowned. 'You guys are stuck in here and *that's* what you want to know?'

Dylan nodded. 'Humour me?'

A few minutes later, Daniels slipped a sheet of paper under the door. He'd copied an explanation from a website.

'I knew it,' Dylan said as he looked at the print-out. 'Look!'

He showed Andy the paper.

'It's called a circumpunct,' Dylan said as he read. '"At the dawn of human history it was used to symbolise the sun. Later it came to be a symbol for gold, the colour of the sun. And in astrology it means sun-day".'

'*Sunday*,' Andy said. 'The day of the attack.'

Dylan nodded. 'We need to tell everyone else.'

But without their phones, they weren't telling anyone anything.

At first the boys were sure Andy's dad would be in any minute. They talked excitedly about the symbols and who might have sent them and how they'd convince Detective Freeman to help. But as minutes piled up into hours and their conversation began to go around in circles, a sense of weariness set in. Despite themselves, the boys snoozed, heads resting on their arms on the conference table.

Dylan woke and rubbed his aching neck. 'Guess we won't be hitting up Laguna Beach today,' he said gloomily.

Andy didn't reply; he was up and peering through the blinds. 'Daniels looks like he's doing an afternoon coffee run,' he said. 'I'll be back in a sec.'

With that, he opened the door and slipped out.

'Hey!' Dylan hissed, jumping to his feet. 'What're you doing?'

Snapping open the blinds answered his question. Andy was crouched by Daniels' desk, collecting their phones from his drawer. A moment later, he scurried back into the conference room and collapsed on the carpet, chest heaving but smiling ear-to-ear.

'Mate,' Dylan said, 'are you crazy?'

'Probably,' Andy grinned. 'But we have to know what's been going on.'

Andy brought up the Games Thinker website.

03:53:59

'Time's running out,' Dylan said, 'for whatever it's counting down to.'

'It'll be about five in the afternoon in Bogotá,' Andy calculated. 'So that means midnight in Athens and Cairo and seven am in Seoul. Not that we should worry about waking people up now.'

Dylan nodded. 'Call all DARE Award winners,' he said softly. 'Link in Andy's phone.'

Seconds later, they had Isabel, Mila, JJ and Zander on their screens. There were greetings all round—and a lot of concern that they still couldn't get through to Yasmin.

'Let me try her again,' Zander said, eyes flicking to make a call on his SmartGlasses. 'Yes, it is ringing!'

Yasmin's face appeared on their shared screens, almost completely in shadow. 'Guys,' she whispered. 'Hi.'

'Thank goodness you are all right,' Zander said. 'We have all been worried.'

'I'm OK,' Yasmin said, 'but the network's been out.'

'Where are you?' Andy asked.

'You won't believe me.'

'Try us,' Dylan said.

Yasmin tilted her phone so they could see her immediate surroundings—ripe green fruit.

'Hiding in a donkey cart under watermelons. I'm heading for the railway station,' she said.

'What? Why?' Isabel asked.

Quickly and quietly, Yasmin told them about her Jackal ordeal, how she'd seen the pyramid attacked, the chase through Cairo and how Miss Chen had arranged her escape from Alexandria. 'But what you really won't believe is that I think the symbols—'

'Predicted what happened,' Zander finished. 'We think that, too.'

'We've sent you texts about it,' JJ added.

'They haven't come through yet,' Yasmin said. 'Quick, tell me before the network drops out again.'

JJ brought Yasmin up to speed on the symbols they'd decoded. Isabel added the information about the pilcrow. Dylan revealed what he'd found out about the circumpunct. Then Yasmin stunned them all with what Sybil had explained about the *lituus*.

'That's it, we've got them all now,' JJ said, holding up his phone screen.

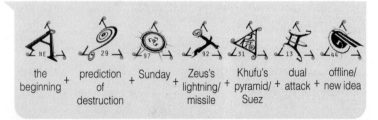

the beginning + prediction of destruction + Sunday + Zeus's lightning/ missile + Khufu's pyramid/ Suez + dual attack + offline/ new idea

'This is freaking me out,' Dylan said.

There were murmurs of agreement.

'Does anyone have any idea about the little arrows around each symbol?' Isabel asked.

No-one did.

'Maybe it's like, I don't know, a brand or something?' Andy said. 'The way we know they're all part of the set?'

Zander shook his head as if dismissing what he considered another lame comment. 'What about this man chasing you?' he asked Yasmin. 'Do you think he is involved?'

Yasmin nodded and shrugged at the same time. 'I don't know. Him appearing at the same time this all happened is definitely strange. But I think I have lost him now.'

'Good,' Zander nodded.

'What is not good,' Mila said softly, 'is the countdown starting again, yes? Will there be another attack when the time runs out?'

No-one wanted to answer that question.

'Yasmin—and Andy and Dylan,' Zander said, 'we wanted to talk to you before deciding whether to tell the authorities about all this. What do you think?'

'Whoever we tell,' said Dylan, 'if they believe us, the first suspect will be Felix.'

'That was my concern,' Zander agreed.

'But him being involved is ridiculous, isn't it?' Dylan asked.

Zander shrugged. 'We seven seem to be the only people who got the symbols.'

Isabel nodded. 'And Felix does have the resources to pull something like this off.'

'But why?' JJ asked. 'Why would he do this?'

'We are not saying he did,' Zander replied. 'Just saying how it might look. Andy, any brilliant ideas?'

Andy snapped out of his thoughts. 'Felix could be connected. Or someone could be setting him up. But in any case, we have to tell someone.'

'But who?' Isabel asked. 'Who can we trust?'

'I don't trust anyone more than my dad,' Andy said.

Zander shook his head. 'Your dad is just a city detective.'

Andy bristled. 'My father is a veteran cop who used to be in army intelligence. He has contacts in the CIA, NSA and FBI. If anyone can put us in touch with the right people, my dad can.'

Zander held up his hands. 'All right. All right. Does everyone agree?'

Everyone did.

'OK,' Andy said. 'Me and Dylan will call you back as soon as we've told him everything.'

The donkey cart came to a stop.

'We're here,' the driver said.

Yasmin climbed out of her hiding spot, thanked the man profusely and ran into the sprawl of Ramses Station. On the outside it seemed like a typical old city building. But the inside terminal resembled a glittering shopping mall. The lower marble floor was lined with plastic white columns. Escalators led to a mezzanine floor of cafes under a ceiling of fake gold-and-blue glass. Everywhere people were huddled and getting the latest updates on the crises from their phones and the wall TVs.

Yasmin hoped Mahmoud was safely back home with her family. In the hours since she'd left the City of the Dead, she'd started to feel confident that she'd eluded Jackal. In a city of millions, plunged into turmoil, surely he couldn't find her now.

Yasmin had to call her family. She had to let them know she was OK. But she also needed her father to go online and buy her a train ticket to Alexandria. Just as she was about to bring up her father's number, her phone rang in her hand. She laughed with relief at the caller ID—it was Mahmoud!

'Brother!' she answered.

But it wasn't Mahmoud who appeared on the phone's screen. It was Jackal.

Peering through the blinds, Andy saw that his dad was at long last striding towards them.

Andy and Dylan hurriedly tucked their phones away.

'I'm sorry you ended up stuck here,' Detective Frank Freeman said as he walked into the conference room.

'Dad, we need to tell you something,' Andy said.

'Whatever you need to say,' he replied, frowning from his son to Dylan. 'You can say to me in the official interview room. Let's go.'

Frank led the boys across the seventh floor to one of the windowless rooms used to interrogate suspects. Furnished with a table and plastic chairs, its walls were bare except for the video camera near the ceiling. Andy knew its flashing red light meant their conversation was being recorded.

'Sit,' Frank ordered, slapping a folder down on the table.

Andy and Dylan glanced at each other and sat.

'So,' Frank said, sipping a coffee, 'the two men in your video came in here first thing this morning.' He let out a tired sigh. 'Wanna know why?'

'To give themselves up?' Andy asked again hopefully.

'No,' Frank said. 'They came in to clear their names and to file charges.'

Andy's mouth dropped open. Dylan looked just as surprised.

'File charges?' Andy said in disbelief.

'Against the two of you.' Frank pressed his hands to his temples like he had a headache. 'Since then I've been doing my best to get you both out of the mess you've made.'

'Mess?' Andy said disbelievingly.

Frank nodded. 'You both have to do exactly what I tell you or—'

The blood had drained from Andy's and Dylan's faces. All thoughts of what they needed to tell Frank were temporarily forgotten.

'Or?' Andy prodded in a small voice.

'Or,' his dad said, 'you're both going to be charged and I'll have to place you under arrest.'

Yasmin had to hold in a scream at the sight of Jackal with his sunglasses and leering smile.

'Hello, Yasmin,' he said. 'Where are you?'

'Where's Mahmoud?' she demanded. 'What have you done with my brother?'

'He's alive ... for now. But he won't be unless you tell me where you are.'

Yasmin wanted to cry. She thought she and Mahmoud had escaped. 'Show me he's OK,' she managed. 'And then I'll tell you where I am.'

Jackal lifted his sunglasses and stared with those cold shark eyes. '*I* give the orders. Tell me where *you* are or I'll show you Mahmoud—dead!'

Yasmin bit her lip. 'I-I-I'm at ... the railway station.'

Jackal smiled smugly. 'Stay there—or Mahmoud dies. Don't call anyone—or Mahmoud dies. Nod if you understand.'

Yasmin nodded.

'Good girl,' he sneered. 'I'll come and find you.'

Yasmin wanted to run. But she couldn't. All she could do was wait for fate to arrive. Her phone rang again. She stared at the caller ID: Home. She pressed the button and her father appeared on the screen.

'Daughter!' he exclaimed. 'Are you all right?'

She nodded.

'You're at the railway station?'

Yasmin nodded. Her heart was breaking. How could she tell him Mahmoud was in danger—and that she was about to be kidnapped?

'Your mother's going online now to buy you a first-class ticket to Alexandria,' Mr Adib said hurriedly. 'The boarding pass will be waiting for you at the ticket office. The train leaves at two-thirty am.'

Yasmin's head spun. How did he know where she was and where she was going? But that didn't matter now. 'Father, listen to me! Mahmoud's been kidnapped—'

'What are you talking about?' her father said. 'Mahmoud just got back. He had to walk the whole way.'

Mr Adib turned his phone to show Mahmoud's smiling face in their lounge room beside her mother and Radha. 'Sister, I am OK,' he said. 'Glad you made it safely.'

'But Jackal called me on your phone!' Yasmin said. 'He said he had you!'

Mahmoud looked like he'd been punched. 'I dropped my phone climbing over a wall. He must've found it and realised our trick! You must hide from him!'

Yasmin ended the call and looked around wildly. She saw that the ticket office was upstairs past a food court. Rushing past people, she pushed her way up the escalator.

Head down, Yasmin hurried towards the ticket office. But a long queue of passengers snaked out the door. If she waited there it would be too easy for Jackal to spot her.

She had to find somewhere to hide while she came up with a plan to get by Jackal and get herself onto the train.

'Excuse me,' a cleaner said as she wiped down a table in front of Yasmin.

Yes! This woman was the answer. Her uniform—blue headscarf, blue apron and blue rubber gloves—made her completely anonymous. Only now did Yasmin notice other women in the same outfit working around the food court. Dressed like that she might be able to evade Jackal and sneak onto the train.

Yasmin hurried to a door marked 'Staff Only'. With a furtive glance around, she pushed her way inside.

Big arms crossed and buzz cut gleaming silver under the fluoro light, Frank's grey eyes bored into Andy across the interrogation-room table. His son now fully appreciated how intimidated suspects must feel in his dad's presence. He felt as though he was shrinking under that hard cop stare.

'Arrest us?' Andy managed in a small voice. He felt as run down as his phone battery. 'You're, like, joking, right?'

Frank looked from his son to Dylan. Perspiration beaded the kid's dark skin and his glasses were fogging up.

'I'm sorry, boys,' Frank said, 'but I'm not.'

'But why?' Dylan asked. 'They're the ones blackmailing kids for money!'

'Things aren't always what they seem,' Frank replied, sliding a folder across to them. 'Take a look.'

The boys huddled together. Andy flipped the file open. Inside were envelopes held together with a rubber band.

'*These* are what they were collecting!' Andy said. 'One of these envelopes had Ethan's money in it.'

Frank let out a weary sigh. 'Look inside any one of them.'

Dylan pulled the top envelope free. He slid out the contents. Instead of a bundle of cash, he held a rectangle of green paper. Beside him, Andy's face was a mess of confusion as his eyes flicked across the white letters edged in black on the sheet.

'"People pile in to ride the air, but underneath's the place where",' Andy read. 'Then there's a bunch of numbers. Are they...?'

'Coordinates,' his father said.

'What the heck does it mean?' Andy asked.

'It's a clue in a game called Geo-Finding,' Frank said. 'People post an initial riddle on an online forum along with some coordinates. Geo-Finders go to that location. If they can work out the puzzle, they'll find the next clue—which leads them to the next location. And so on.'

Dylan studied the riddle and its coordinates. 'So, what is this pointing to?'

'The coordinates are for the Santa Monica Pier Ferris wheel,' said Frank. 'But the rhyme is a play on words that tells you where to look.' He pointed at the riddle on the paper. 'See here, "pile in", like "pylon"? The next envelope was taped to a pylon underneath the boardwalk.'

Andy frowned so hard it hurt. Dylan pulled out another yellow envelope. Same green rectangle, another rhyming riddle printed in white letters with black borders.

'"High up above the smog and cars, is the best place in Hollywood to see the stars".' he read. '"Rest your feet and take a seat!" Thirty-four point one one eight six degrees north...'

Andy couldn't get his head around any of this. But what he was hearing still made him feel sick to the stomach.

'"People gather from all around in the dead centre of town. You won't waste hours if you check the flowers",'

Dylan read from another green rectangle before rattling off more coordinates.

Andy let out a groan. Now he understood. Those were riddles pointing to Griffith Observatory and Hollywood Forever Cemetery.

He shook his head. 'Dad, Bald Guy and Beard Dude must've put these green paper clues in *after* they took the money out. You know, to use as a cover story!'

Dylan clicked his fingers. 'That's it! Detective Freeman, that *has* to be what happened.'

Frank shook his head. 'These men have been Geo-Finders for years. I've spent half the day checking their stories. You couldn't have picked two more upstanding citizens to accuse of intimidation and extortion. Larry Baker, your "Beard Dude", teaches English at Beverly Hills High. Tony Jackson, "Bald Guy", is the reverend at St Mark's in Inglewood.'

The boys swapped mortified looks. They had accused a *teacher* and a *pastor* in a *Scoop* story already seen by one million people? This was a *disaster!* And Felix Scott himself had endorsed the story in a tweet.

Frank slid another piece of paper out from the folder. The boys forced themselves to look at it. It was a police incident report from officers who attended a call at Hollywood Forever Cemetery the previous evening.

'Larry and Tony's story checks out. *They* phoned *us* to report vandals.'

'Vandals?' Andy gulped.

'Apparently you boys smashed a statue at the cemetery.

That wasn't in your *Scoop* video, was it?'

'No, no,' Dylan said, shaking his head. 'But it was an *accident.*'

Frank frowned. 'You did run off, though?'

'Because they chased us!' Andy said. 'We thought they knew we had busted them!

'I don't understand,' he continued, rubbing his jaw. 'Ethan told me he was being threatened. That he had to drop the money at the Griffith Observatory. Dad, you've *seen* the video!'

Frank slid a photo from the folder. It was a still from the *Scoop* video, showing Ethan, with his mop of red hair and nerd glasses. 'That could be a wig and those spectacles could be fake,' he said. 'We have no idea what he really looks like, do we? This guy, without a surname, whose phone is disconnected.'

Andy fumed. His dad was right. He'd been so eager to believe that he hadn't for a moment questioned whether Ethan was for real.

With a nod, Andy pulled out his wallet and fanned out a few ten-dollar bills. Their green colour, white lettering and black edging were similar to the envelope clues.

'From a distance, it looked like Bald Guy and Beard Dude were retrieving cash,' Andy said. 'Ethan must have switched the envelopes—no wonder he didn't want me to open it!'

Dylan nodded. 'Mate, I reckon you and I were—'

'Set up,' Andy finished.

Andy's shoulders slumped. Dylan blew a frustrated breath at the ceiling.

Frank rubbed his whiskery cheek. 'You've made some enemies with *Scoop*, son, and what better way to discredit you than by getting you to fall for a hoax?'

Andy had to admit that was possible. 'So what now? Are you really going to arrest us both?'

Frank held up a finger. 'I didn't say I *was* arresting you. I said I'd *have* to arrest you if you don't do exactly as I say.'

The boys saw a faint light at the end of the tunnel.

'So,' Andy ventured, 'what do we have to do?'

Frank cracked his knuckles, stared from his son to Dylan and then back to Andy. 'Boys,' he said, 'you're not going to like this one bit.'

Yasmin wanted to cry. Since rushing into the storeroom, she'd tried to open two dozen lockers. She was sure that one of them had to hold a cleaner's uniform that'd provide her with the disguise she needed to get across the railway station undetected by Jackal. But every locker lived up to its name: locked! She was running out of time. The train was leaving in just a few minutes. She didn't have a way to avoid Jackal or to get onto the train.

Then Yasmin saw her salvation. A big hamper at the back of the room beneath a sign that read LAUNDRY. She scrambled across to it and gave a little whoop of triumph. The hamper was a treasure chest of discarded uniforms awaiting washing. Beside it was a tub of gloves. Without worrying about the smell or the stains, Yasmin whipped off her green scarf and stuffed it into her pocket. She put on a blue scarf, threw a cleaning apron over her top and stretched gloves over her fingers. To complete her look, Yasmin commandeered a trolley standing by the back wall that was loaded with sprays and wipes.

'What're you doing?' a voice said behind her.

Yasmin turned slowly. A security guard stood in the doorway. He munched on a cheeseburger, belly straining against his shirt. Smiling, Yasmin pushed the trolley towards him. She saw his name badge on his shirt—Benny.

'Just about to start my shift, Benny,' she said.

Benny wiped his mouth. 'I don't know you,' he said. 'I know all the cleaners.'

'I, uh, just started,' Yasmin said. 'Today's my first day.'

'I'll still need to see your ID badge,' he said.

Yasmin slapped her gloved hand to her forehead. 'I left it at home.'

As soon as the words left her mouth she realised her mistake, and saw the guard had too.

Benny tossed his wrapper into a bin. 'I thought today was your first day,' he said, reaching for the radio hanging on his belt. 'I've got to check you out wi—'

The guard's eyes flashed with surprise and he frowned like he was confused. When he opened his mouth, blood trickled out and down his chin. He let out a wheeze and fell forwards with a thump.

Jackal stood there, holding a bloodied knife. He closed the door and stepped over Benny's body. 'See what you made me do,' he said with a cold smirk.

Yasmin's hands gripped the trolley's handles. She wondered whether she could rush Jackal with it.

'This little chase of ours has been fun,' he said, 'but I've had enough now. Come with me and you won't get hurt.'

'Like *he* didn't get hurt?' Yasmin said looking at poor Benny's bleeding body. 'You won't let me live. I've seen too much. I've seen your face.'

Jackal stepped closer. 'Good point,' he said, lifting his sunglasses, revealing dark eyes absolutely without pity.

'But I can get a ransom and then kill you anyway.'

Yasmin didn't have a comeback for that. She didn't need one.

Her hand flew to a spray bottle.

Jackal screamed as she squirted cleaning chemicals into his eyes. He whirled and slashed blindly with the knife. That's when Yasmin shoved the trolley forwards, slamming him into a wall of lockers. She ran to the door, tore off the cleaner's uniform, bolted across the food court and bounded down the escalator steps.

'The train to Alexandria will be departing in four minutes,' a pleasant voice said from the station's speakers. 'All passengers please make your way to platform three.'

Yasmin broke into a sprint.

Platform three was at the other end of the station!

'Look,' Frank said, 'Larry and Tony know you were set up—and realise they were, too.'

'They do?' asked Andy.

'They were?' Dylan added.

Frank nodded. 'The Geo-Finder member who set the clues was anonymous and they have since deleted their account without a trace. But that doesn't change the fact that Larry and Tony could press charges. Given how much damage you've done to their reputations, you could end up in juvenile detention.'

Andy and Dylan traded fearful looks, imagining themselves behind bars.

'Luckily,' Frank continued, 'they're reasonable guys. They both work with kids. They don't want your lives ruined. Besides, they're not squeaky clean in this.'

'They're not?' Andy asked, as Dylan's eyebrows shot up.

Frank nodded. 'They *were* trespassing in Hollywood Forever Cemetery. Just because a fellow Geo-Finder regularly leaves a gate unlocked doesn't make it legal to go inside. They didn't admit to that when they made their anonymous tip-off about seeing vandals. It's not much, but it's all the leverage I've got.'

Andy nodded. He'd take whatever hope was offered. 'So, what now, Dad?'

Frank drained his coffee cup and tossed it in the bin. 'I've told them I won't file trespass charges against them. They've agreed to drop the charges against you if . . .'

The boys looked at each other.

'If?' Andy asked.

'If you apologise,' Frank said.

The boys looked at each other with delight. This could all go away that easily?

'Sure,' said Andy. 'I feel terrible about what's happened.'

'That's it?' asked Dylan. 'They just want us to say "sorry"?'

Frank shook his head slowly. 'Not just say it—vlog it. They want a personal apology. But they also want a public apology. They want you both to say sorry on video and post it to *Scoop*.'

Silence descended in the interrogation room.

Andy knew what that would mean for him and for *Scoop*. He also knew he had no choice. But the least he could do was make sure Dylan didn't share the blame.

'OK,' Andy said finally. 'But just me. It's my website. It was my idea.'

'No way, mate,' Dylan said. 'We're in this together.'

'I'm impressed by your loyalty,' Frank said, 'but you both have to make the video. And Larry and Tony want the apology seen by as many people as saw the accusation, so they need Felix Scott to acknowledge it with a follow-up tweet. Do you think he'll do that?'

Andy nodded. But he hated to think how Felix would react to such public embarrassment.

Frank stood up. 'I'll get your phones from Daniels so you can film the apology and contact Felix.'

'Um, Dad?' Andy said, sheepishly, pulling his InfiniFone from his camo pants pocket. He glanced at Dylan, who produced his phone from the pocket of his Hawaiian shirt.

Frank's eyes hardened. 'I told Officer Daniels to confiscate those.'

'He did,' Andy admitted. 'But I kinda, er, liberated them from his desk.'

His father scowled but swallowed his anger. 'First trespass and now stealing police evidence? When this is all over, you and I are going to have a serious talk.'

Andy nodded, eyes downcast. 'Yes, sir.'

Frank left and the boys looked at each other.

'Mate, do you reckon we were set up by someone with a grudge against *Scoop*?' Dylan asked.

'Could be,' Andy said. 'Like I said, I've had death threats before because of my stories.'

'Who do you think Ethan really was?' Dylan asked.

'Dunno.' Andy threw back his chair and prowled the room. 'I feel so ... dumb,' he murmured, kicking at a skirting board with a sneaker.

'Well,' Dylan said, raking his fingers through his dreadlocks, 'that makes us dumb and dumber because I fell for Ethan's whole nerd act.'

Andy let out a little laugh.

'Was there *anything* about him that was familiar?' Dylan asked.

'Dude, he could've been anyone. He might've even been hired to play the part.'

'Hired?' Dylan said, on his feet now, fists balled in the pockets of his khaki trousers as he circled the table. 'What do you mean?'

Andy shrugged. 'Someone contacts these Geo-Finders and dangles a clue. Then sets up the envelopes and gets "Ethan" to come to us with a story that's right up *Scoop*'s alley. All he has to do is hand over an envelope and disappear. You and me, and this Larry and Tony, do the rest, without even realising it.'

Dylan nodded. 'I guess there's plenty of desperate young actors in Hollywood who'd do something like that.'

'That's how your parents started out, right?' Andy joked.

But instead of laughing, Dylan smacked a hand to his forehead. 'Maybe this didn't have anything to do with your old *Scoop* stories,' he said, grabbing the envelopes left on the table. 'Remember what Bald Guy said at the observatory?'

Andy thought a moment. '"Five down, two to go"?'

Dylan fanned out the envelopes.

'Seven envelopes!' Andy said.

Dylan nodded. '*Seven* envelopes, *seven* coordinates, *seven* weird riddles. No way that's a coincidence, right?'

'Can't be. Now it makes more sense. This isn't about payback.'

Andy punched a fist into his palm with a smack! 'It's to stop me using *Scoop* to turn the signs into a story! I mean, who'd believe me now I've fallen for a massive hoax, right?'

'*We*,' Dylan said. '*We* fell for it.'

Andy nodded. 'Well, if *we* try to use *Scoop* to tell anyone about the signs now, they'll think we're making it up.'

Dylan tapped a finger to his head. 'Or that we're a couple of kangaroos short in the top paddock.'

Andy managed a grin. 'I'd be surprised if even my dad believes us.'

'We've gotta try to convince him,' Dylan said. 'These envelopes, the set-up, he's gotta see it's for real, yeah?'

'I hope so,' Andy said. 'But he's not gonna listen to a thing we say until we've made that apology video.'

The boys stood side by side and filmed themselves saying sorry for running the story.

With a minute to go, Yasmin forced herself to slow down as she reached the gate to platform three.

A neatly uniformed guard was checking a woman's ticket against his passenger list. 'Take care, madam,' he said, waving her through before his eyes skipped to Yasmin. 'Boarding pass, please, miss.'

'I'm sorry,' Yasmin said breathlessly, 'but I haven't had time to pick it up. With all the traffic out there, I barely made it here.'

The guard wrinkled his mouth. 'Well, you'll have to get it and catch a later train,' he said. 'You must understand that security is a big priority today. I have to do my job.'

Yasmin burst into tears. She didn't have to fake it. Not only had today's events taken their toll but getting on this train was her only chance of getting away from here alive!

The guard shifted awkwardly. 'Miss, please, don't cry,' he said quietly. 'Have you got ID?'

Snuffling, Yasmin handed over her passport. The man studied it and checked his passenger list.

'Yasmin Adib, first class, seat 5C,' he said. 'Please go through. Hurry!'

'Really?' she asked, wiping her eyes.

He nodded. 'Go before I change my mind. Next!'

Yasmin rushed along the busy platform to the first-class

carriage directly behind the engines that would pull the long train north to Alexandria. She climbed aboard and took her seat, anxiously looking through the window, expecting to see Jackal's leering face appear at any moment. Yasmin counted down seconds that seemed to take hours.

There was a long whistle and the cry of 'All aboard!'

A horn blared, the carriage lurched forward and then Cairo's railway station was sliding away. The train settled into a reassuring rumbling rhythm as it picked up speed. Yasmin relaxed a little into her seat.

Behind her women talked in low voices about the day's events.

Yasmin wondered what they would say if she told them what she knew. That the attacks were part of a larger plot. That there might be more to come. That she was somehow caught up in it. She thought the women would probably say she was crazy. Yasmin hoped Andy's dad didn't have that reaction. She hoped the detective believed his son and that his contacts could ensure nothing else terrible happened.

Thinking of Andy's dad made Yasmin realise she still hadn't let her own father know she was all right. She pulled out her phone and tapped out a quick text.

> Made the train safely.
> I'll call you from Alexandria.
> Love, Yasmin

Then she texted Miss Chen.

> On board train to Alexandria
> ETA 3 hours

Yasmin nearly screamed when she saw a shadow loom over her reflection in the window.

Terrified, she turned—and then sighed with relief.

'Miss?'

The blinking man standing in the aisle looked meek and mild. He held out his boarding pass.

'I think you're in my seat,' he said.

Yasmin laughed.

'See—5D,' he said. 'Window.'

'Of course,' she said. 'I'm sorry.'

They shuffled around and the man took his seat and promptly went to sleep.

As he snored, Yasmin realised something awful. Her name was on the passenger list! If Jackal had gotten access to it, then he'd know not only the train she had boarded but which carriage she was in and even which seat she occupied.

With the train slowing as it came to a suburban station, Yasmin suddenly felt very vulnerable.

She had to find a place to hide.

As soon as they had finished filming their apology, Andy brought up the Games Thinker website.

0:00:21

Every muscle tensed, the boys stood together and watched the website countdown run out.

'It's freaky knowing there might be another attack somewhere,' Andy said, 'and not being able to do a thing to stop it.'

Dylan swallowed hard.

00:00:00

Without missing a beat, the screen changed.

www.gamesthinker.com

YOU EVEN DREAM OF PAST SINCE THE SECOND SIGN
12:57:00

'The Second Sign?' Dylan mused.

Equally puzzling was the new message that had appeared above the timer.

Before Andy could reply, his and Dylan's phones vibrated with incoming texts.

The boys eyed their screens nervously.

'I'll go first,' Andy said. 'Open text.'

 'Another symbol?' he said.

'Open text,' Dylan said.

'What are they?' he asked when his symbol was revealed.

'I don't know,' Andy said. 'But the pattern's repeating—countdown, phrase, symbols. It's what the website says: The Second Sign.'

As the train rattled through the night to Alexandria, Yasmin huddled behind a menu in the dining carriage. This wasn't any sort of hiding place but at least she wasn't a sitting duck in her assigned seat.

'Miss, can I take your order yet?' a tired waiter asked. 'These tables are for paying customers.'

'Still deciding,' she said, smiling apologetically. 'Just another minute, OK?'

The man sighed and, with a backwards glance, attended to another table.

Yasmin's phone vibrated in her pocket as it received a text. Imagining all sorts of horrible threats from Jackal, she couldn't bring herself to look at it.

Instead, she jumped up and pushed past the waiter with a quick 'sorry, not hungry'. She rushed into the next carriage. Every seat was filled. There was nowhere to hide. Sleepy passengers blinked as she hurried past them. Ahead of her, at the end of the carriage, a uniformed porter pushed a big trolley of suitcases to a baggage room. This was her chance! Yasmin crept up on him. When the porter unlocked the door, she weaved around him, slipped inside and ducked down behind a big crate. Not daring to breathe, she listened as the man arranged luggage. Yasmin didn't exhale until he'd left and turned the key in the lock.

In the darkness, she finally dared to check her phone.

'Oh, no.' She gazed at her screen in shock. 'Oh, *no*.'

What she saw wasn't a taunting text from Jackal. It was far, far worse.

The meaning of the symbol was impossible to miss.
Death.

Yasmin went to the Games Thinker website, and saw the new countdown and message.

The Second Sign? It was starting all over again! What was this diabolical game? She had no idea. But what was clear was that in just over a dozen hours there'd be another deadly attack somewhere in the world.

'Call DARE Award winners,' she whispered.

Soon all seven were linked up.

'I got another symbol,' Zander said, 'right at the moment the clock went to zero. Did everyone else get one, too?'

Yasmin nodded.

'This,' she said softly, sharing the terrifying skull image, 'is what I got.'

Their eyes widened as it hit their phones.

'What did everyone else get?' Yasmin asked.

Everyone shared theirs quickly.

'The new message on the Games Thinker site,' Dylan said. 'Does it mean anything to anybody?'

'Events for you as mind peace, you even dream of past since,' JJ said. 'Combining them sounds like a song lyric. Anyone know it?'

'It sorta rhymes,' Isabel said. 'But no.'

'I'll keep trying,' JJ said.

'The symbols,' Mila said, 'does anyone know what is the meaning of theirs?'

'Mine is obvious,' Yasmin said, trying to keep the fear from her voice. 'Death.'

'I think mine's a moon, as in Moon-day, Monday,' JJ said. 'That's when the timer runs out.'

'Mine looks like a No Right Turn sign,' Andy said.

'Mine looks like a bird,' Mila observed.

'Mine could be a clock,' Dylan added.

'The others?' Yasmin asked.

'I don't know,' JJ said. 'And there are no coordinates to help figure out which order they go in.'

'Andy,' Isabel said, 'have you told your dad yet?'

'I'm about to,' he replied, with a sideways glance at Dylan. 'Things here have been complicated.'

Zander shook his head, as if he'd expected such an answer, before he turned a concerned frown to Yasmin. 'Where are you?' he asked.

'Hiding in the baggage room on the train to Alexandria,' she whispered.

'Hiding?' he said. 'Is that crooked cop *still* after you?'

Yasmin gulped and wiped a tear from her cheek. 'I don't know. But . . .' She choked back a sob. 'H-h-he killed a security guard right in front of me at the railway station.'

Her friends gasped.

Yasmin's brown eyes shimmered. 'I think he's—'

She didn't dare breathe. There were voices outside the baggage room!

'I'm a detective,' Jackal was saying just on the other side of the door. 'I'm looking for a dangerous female who might've just stabbed a man at the station.'

Yasmin wanted to scream. Instead she set her phone to silent.

She had seconds to find a concealed spot.

'I'm not allowed to open this for anyone,' the porter protested outside the door.

'But I'm *not* just anyone,' Jackal said. 'This is official police business. Give me the key and get out of here.'

Jackal slipped inside and closed the door behind him. He shone his flashlight around the dim room, over suit-cases and boxes. Finally, the beam came to rest on the crate.

'Yasmin, Yasmin, Yasmin,' Jackal said. 'I saw your name on the passenger list. Since I caught up with the train, I've searched every carriage. This is the last place left. So ... out you come.'

The night air whipping around her, Yasmin peered down through the skylight. Jackal was directly beneath her. If he looked up, she'd be caught. But she was too scared to let go of the skylight frame and move farther along the carriage's roof. At this speed, she'd be killed if she fell from the train. Just climbing up the shelves and pushing her way out here had taken every bit of courage she had.

Answered with silence, Jackal prowled around the crate. Yasmin heard him curse in frustration. A moment later, he started opening bigger suitcases, as though she might've tucked herself in among a stranger's clothes. He let out a whistle when he found rings and a necklace in one bag and swiftly pocketed the jewellery. Just over his head, Yasmin hoped this score was enough to satisfy his greed.

It seemed to be because, after a final look around, Jackal left and closed the door behind him.

Yasmin was building up the courage to climb down through the skylight when she saw the baggage room door swing open again.

Beneath her, Jackal stepped back into the room.

He shone his torch at the shelves. She saw his grin in the glow of his flashlight.

Yasmin knew what he was looking at. She'd left dusty footprints on the shelves when she'd used them as a ladder to get to the skylight.

Jackal looked up and saw her peering down.

'Hi, Yasmin,' he said. 'Mind if I join you?'

'Cairo–Alexandria train,' the Signmaker said, 'find and zoom in.'

In a split second, the HoloSpace showed a satellite image of the train racing through the Egyptian night. There were two figures on the roof of a middle carriage.

'Acquire heat signatures and zoom.'

The images showed Yasmin backing away from Jackal's gun as the countryside whizzed by. The Signmaker had saved the girl once, sending that AutoDrive car into the cop's motorbike back on the Cairo bridge, but that effort would've been in vain if she died now.

There were only seconds to do something—and it would have to be something drastic.

'Access signals and rail network.'

The command went out and a moment later the Signmaker had control of the Cairo–Alexandria Express from the security of the golden-lit secret headquarters.

'Digitise voice to Yasmin Adib. Disengage Yasmin Adib silent phone function.'

Yasmin knew she was going to die. Either she'd jump to her death or Jackal would shoot her.

'This could've been easy,' Jackal growled, pistol aimed right at her heart. If he was afraid of falling, he didn't show it as he staggered towards her. 'You could've lived. Things didn't have to be this way.'

Jackal seethed, touching his fingers to his face. 'Look at what you did to me. Just look!'

By the moonlight, Yasmin saw where the skin around his eyes was red and puffy. As wrong as it was to hurt anyone, she silently wished he'd suffered more chemical damage. If she had really blinded him, he wouldn't be about to kill her.

Mouth dry, heart hammering, Yasmin glanced away from Jackal to the dark countryside blurring by on either side of the speeding train. If she jumped, her body would be broken beyond belief. It was horrible, but it would deny the man the satisfaction of killing her.

As if reading her mind, he stepped closer. 'There's nowhere to hide this time.' Squinting through burning eyes, Jackal chuckled humourlessly. 'You're going to die.'

Anger surged through Yasmin. This was so unfair. In just hours, she'd gone from being a DARE Award winner, whose life was to be filled with adventure and opportunity, to a desperate fugitive, with her life being measured in seconds. Only one word echoed in her mind: Why? Why had Jackal really been sent at the same time she and her friends had received the mysterious symbols? Why had Egypt been attacked? There *had* to be a connection. She had to know the truth. Why did she have to die? But when Yasmin opened her mouth to demand an answer, the only sound was the loud ringtone of her phone bleating at top volume in her pocket.

'Ha!' Jackal said. 'Yasmin can't answer the phone right now because—'

But she didn't need to. Her phone had accepted the call and switched to speaker.

'Get down and hold on!' a computerised voice commanded loudly. 'Now!'

Yasmin didn't stop to think.

She dropped to the roof, hands grabbing the pipes on either side of her.

'Hey, what—' Jackal said.

Whatever he said after that was lost in the screech of brakes as the train shuddered beneath them.

Jackal screamed as he shot forwards, crunching into the carriage roof before being flung away into the darkness.

For a moment, Yasmin wondered if he'd survived.

Then all she knew was she was losing her grip on the pipes as the train began to buck off the tracks beneath her.